The Dagger of Bahyel

The First Elf Adventure

Sandra McPherson

Illustrated by Dana M. Richardi

authorHOUSE®

AuthorHouse™
1663 Liberty Drive
Bloomington, IN 47403
www.authorhouse.com
Phone: 1-800-839-8640

Published by AuthorHouse 2/7/2013

ISBN: 978-1-4817-1341-2 (sc)
ISBN: 978-1-4817-1342-9 (hc)
ISBN: 978-1-4817-1343-6 (e)

Library of Congress Control Number: 2013902296

Table of Contents

Map of the Realm

Chapter 1

GETTING READY FOR WINTER

It was a bright, sunshiny, crisp air kind of day. Winter would be here soon, but today the leaves were yellow and orange and red and every hue in between. It was near the end of the harvest season and Gidley and his friends Casha and Bellina were in the Lega Woods filling baskets with the very large acorns that grew in those woods.

"Ooh, it's so hard to find the acorns with all these leaves," Casha cried.

"I know, but we have to get as many as we can today," Gidley reminded her.

"What do the Fairies do with all these acorns, anyway?" asked Bellina.

"Well, the Fairies use the acorn caps for dishes. Bowls are made from the whole ones. The woodworker Elves clean and polish them, just as they are, although some are stained with berry juice and other natural dyes. Those are for the more important Fairies. Plates are made by rubbing them on rocks to grind down the rims until they are almost flat. I guess they break a lot doing that, plus, there are a lot of Fairies."

"Ooh, thanks for the history lesson, Gidley."

"Yeah," Casha said. "You're sooo smart."

"Hey, you asked. I was only trying to help. I thought maybe you girls

1

could use the information. Ouch!" Casha hit him right between the eyes with an acorn.

"Good shot!" Bellina said, half laughing, half serious.

"You could put someone's eye out doing that," Gidley said indignantly. "Why do you two always have to end up hurting me?"

"I'm sorry, really," Casha giggled. "I just meant to toss it near you. I guess I'm a worse shot than I thought. I tried to miss!" She burst out laughing and was joined by Bellina. This was too much for Gidley and he started pelting them both with acorns as they ran for their lives, laughing and taunting him.

Of course, Gidley didn't really try to hit them. Well, not *too* hard. He would never do anything to hurt anyone, especially Casha, whom he thought was the most beautiful Elf in Sharrock. She was just a little over three feet, seven inches tall and very slim. She had softly curled, golden, blond hair that hung to her waist and violet-blue eyes. She was the best singer in the country and she danced as though her feet were encased in cloud puffs. They had been friends all their lives and one day he was going to marry her. Of course, they would probably have to let Bellina live with them. She also, was the best friend of both of them and exactly the opposite of Casha. She too, was beautiful, but her hair was so dark it was almost black and she always put it in one big, fat braid, which she wore draped over her right shoulder. She had dark, hazel eyes that sparkled when she laughed. Bellina was three feet, eight inches tall and also slim. She and Casha often danced together, but Bellina played the flute and hardly ever sang.

Gidley played the flute and with his dark brown hair and deep green eyes, kept all the female Elves interested. He stood almost four feet tall and was considered to be the most handsome Elf for miles around. He didn't sing or dance, but no one minded.

They ran down near the Teld Stream and all three dropped down near the water's edge, panting and laughing.

"You made me drop all my acorns," Bellina exclaimed, looking down at her now empty basket.

"Well, looks like you better get going. Queen Findra promised to have lots of dishes for Queen Sennabelle by the end of the week and today is our day to gather them.

We can't disappoint the Queen."

"Right. Come on, Bellina," Casha said. "I'll help you. I don't know why we put up with him anyway." She gave Gidley a wink, as she turned and skipped away to help fill Bellina's basket, again.

Gidley, Casha and Bellina in the Lega Woods

Gidley followed to help, too. It really wouldn't do to let Bellina incur the wrath of Queen Findra. She wasn't a mean Queen, but she demanded absolute respect and no one ever disobeyed her. No one wanted to. They all loved her and she was fiercely protective of all her Elves. However, not getting enough dishes for the fairies' Queen Sennabelle, would make Queen Findra look bad and no one wanted that, especially not these three. It was the first year they were out on their own, together, to collect acorns. They were usually with a larger group of friends, gathering berries and herbs, so they really wanted to make a good impression.

This courtesy to Queen Sennabelle started a long time ago when Sharrock was under attack by evil Elves from a far off realm. The Fairies came from Kellenshire and helped during the battle. The Fairies are tiny creatures, but they have magical powers and they have the ability to fly. They were a great asset during the battle, because they were able to act as messengers, back and forth between Queen Findra and the battlefield. With the fairies' help, the Elves of Sharrock were able to keep their army informed of all battle plans and strategies.

They won that war and when Queen Findra asked what she could do to repay the Fairies for their help, Queen Sennabelle revealed how difficult it was for the tiny Fairies, who were only between three and six inches tall, to hunt, gather, and fashion the acorn caps into usable dishes. So now, each year the Elves do it for them. The Elves also gather fruit and nuts and preserve them, usually by drying, and provide food sources for themselves and the Fairies for winter. The Fairies keep a strict look out at the borders, for intruders, and also look for sources of honey and berries. Much of the winter clothing for the wealthy Elves comes from the Fairies. They weave a lightweight cloth, known as Fairy silk, that is extremely warm.

They work well together and they all stay well fed and safe. They are great neighbors!

After filling Bellina's basket once again, the three friends started back toward home.

Suddenly, Gidley stopped and held his hand up for the girls to stop talking. He cocked his head to listen.

"What is it?" asked Casha.

"Shhh! I thought I heard someone scream."

"Where?" asked Bellina.

"Shhh! How can I hear, if you two keep chattering," Gidley said, as he motioned them to stay back. He advanced to the edge of a stand of trees.

Listening again, he heard a scream and voices coming from the wooded area ahead.

"Stay here, I think someone's in trouble." He ran forward pulling his small dagger, from its sheath.

Not being ones to listen to Gidley or to remain somewhere, when there was adventure elsewhere, both girls hesitated a few minutes and then threw down their baskets of acorns and ran after him.

When they finally caught up to Gidley they both let out small sounds of surprise. It seemed that a large branch had broken off from a tree and had fallen, pinning an old Elf to the ground. His head was bleeding and he wasn't moving. Two young Elves, one boy and one girl, were crying and calling '*Ga-pa, ga-pa*', over and over.

Most startling, however, was that Gidley was engaged in a battle for his life against a deadly lupode, a wolflike creature, who usually inhabited the land further north. Why a lupode was here in the woods of Sharrock they could not guess, but it was clear he *was* here and Gidley needed help.

Both girls ran forward just as Gidley thrust his dagger into the heart of the creature, as it sprang forth, in an attempt to kill Gidley.

With the lupode lying at his feet, breathing its last breath, Gidley turned his attention to the old Elf pinned under the fallen branch.

Casha and Bellina knew that Gidley wasn't going to be able to move the large branch alone, so they rushed forward to help.

Casha called to the children to keep back and not to panic, although she felt pretty scared and panicky herself, at that moment.

"Bellina, grab the end over there and pull towards me," Gidley shouted. "Casha, come here and help me pull this way."

As the branch started to move, the old Elf groaned and opened his eyes.

"He may be really hurt, but he's not dead," Bellina said with relief.

"How can we get him back home, even when we free him?" Casha asked.

"Someone will have to go get help," Gidley decided. "I think you two should stay here with the little ones and comfort the old Elf. I can run the fastest, so I'll go back to Sharrocktown for help."

"Come let's move this branch off of him."

Putting all the strength they could muster, they pulled and pulled and finally freed the old Elf. The children ran to him and began to comfort him, as he lay moaning.

Gidley took off at a fast run toward town and help.

"Casha, I think we can keep us and the children calm, if I play my flute and you sing along," Bellina suggested.

"Good idea," Casha responded. "It won't take Gidley long to get help. He runs like the wind."

Very shortly, voices could be heard coming towards them. Gidley had indeed run like the wind and three of their friends, riding on their ponies, were headed to where the old Elf lay.

They had brought along a leather pouch filled with *vita* that the elves were famous for in their realm. The fairies and elves make it from magic water, honey and herbs. One good drink and the old Elf quieted right down. Vita has special properties to heal and calm, so that the Elves were able to lift the old Elf onto a sling made from two poles covered with leather. Once it was fastened to Dira's pony they were able to drag him, quickly but gently, back to Sharrocktown for medical attention.

Casha and Bellina helped the two little ones on to the other two ponies and the other riders took off with them, following their grandfather.

Gidley had a huge grin on his face. "We sure did our good deed for the day!"

Casha and Bellina smiled and agreed with him.

"Although," said Casha, "I'm afraid we have all lost our acorns."

"Here we go again," Bellina sighed.

"We had better hurry," Gidley said. "It's going to be dark soon and it's starting to get cold."

"That old Elf sure was lucky you heard the kids scream," Bellina said. "He may not have made it through the cold night, even if the lupode hadn't threatened to kill them all.

Chapter 2

THE BREAKFAST

Gidley awoke to the sound of his name being called. He lay there and listened a minute.

"No, I guess I was dreaming. No, I definitely hear my name. It sounds like Bellina and Casha. Why would they be up so early?" Gidley climbed out of bed and ran to the window. There was Casha and Bellina standing near the garden with one of the Queen's guardsmen. 'Why is he here?' Gidley wondered out loud.

"Hello, Mr. Gidley. Please come down at once and join us," the guard called.

"I, I can't. I'm not dressed. You woke me up," Gidley said, confused.

"Please, dress quickly. Her Majesty, Queen Findra awaits you," the guard called up to him.

"Queen Findra? The Queen wants to see *me*?" Gidley exclaimed. "Why?" But deep down inside he knew why. They had failed to gather enough acorns yesterday and the Queen was probably mad. They had a real good excuse, however, so Gidley knew they wouldn't get into too much trouble. Besides they could volunteer to go again today. He was almost ready for winter and he knew the girls were even more diligent than he was. If he felt ready, he knew they would be.

"Okay, be right down," Gidley called out cheerfully. He didn't feel cheerful, however.

After 'good mornings' to his two best friends and to the very nice guard, they all set out for the palace.

The palace was set on a rock ledge, which was the highest elevation in the middle of Sharrocktown, the ruling town of Sharrock. Sharrock was one of the largest Kingdoms of Elves, in that part of the world. It was peaceful and quiet and the surrounding kingdoms were all on good terms. The wars and battles were long over.

Sharrock was made up of small towns, on mostly flat, level land. The children, animals and crops were raised in a land of rich, fertile soil that supported many farms. The gentle, streams, stands of tall, majestic trees and fields of wild flowers made for a quiet place to live a wonderful life. Even winters here, although cold and snowy, weren't as harsh as they were in the kingdoms farther north.

The palace was built of splendid white marble and the finest wood and it could be seen from almost anywhere in Sharrocktown. The Queen's flag, a gold dragon on a white background, flew from the tower. The palace was surrounded by a high wall and during a war or dangerous situation all of the Elves of Sharrock could be brought inside. With the gates closed they were safe and the Queen's guards could defend them and their Queen. Very few Elves ever got to go inside the palace itself; however, they were all frequently in the courtyard, at the front of the palace, under the balcony. It was from this balcony that Queen Findra made all of her important announcements.

Upon reaching the courtyard, all three friends stopped and looked up at the balcony. The guard surprised them by asking them to hurry along. They followed behind and gave each other inquisitive looks. Maybe they were in more trouble, than Gidley had first thought.

The guard ushered them into a large room, brightly lit with candles. The walls were covered with rich fabrics and there were the most lavish furnishings they had ever seen. This was not at all like the small rooms in the tiny cottages, that most Elves were used to living in.

"My dear subjects and heroes, please approach the throne," Queen Findra intoned. "Guard, thank you. You may leave now."

The three friends approached and knelt before the Queen. They felt not at all like heroes. Queen Findra only stood three feet, six inches tall, but she was still a commanding presence. This morning she was dressed in a simple gown of pale blue, her dark brown hair long and flowing; a golden crown on her head.

"Please rise. I have heard of your deeds of yesterday in the forest. I am pleased to have such brave subjects. I expect my guards and soldiers to do brave deeds. It is their job and they are dedicated, but for mere Elves such as you three, to be put into such danger to spare others, ah, I am most pleased. You may not be aware of exactly whom you have saved."

"No Your Majesty." Casha was the bravest today and the first to speak directly to the Queen.

The other two mumbled 'no' and fell silent.

Queen Findra continued, "I didn't think so. The elderly Elf is Atilol. Years ago during the horrible war with the Elves from Dordom, Atilol and his young son, Andely, served in my army. Andely was a fine Elf and very good soldier, better than most. He helped his father lead the army. He was brave and fought to his death. Atilol was grief stricken over Andely's death, but that didn't prevent him from continuing to fight and finally help win the war.

When Atilol returned home, he found that his wife had also been killed by a group of marauding soldiers. Their young daughter had been spared and Atilol raised her on a farm outside of Sharrocktown. He was fiercely proud of his son's bravery, but was so broken hearted over his wife and son's deaths that he became a recluse. He was one of our greatest heroes, but sadly, we rarely see him now. He lives with his daughter and her two children, whom you met yesterday. It seems the daughter was so busy with winter preparations that Atilol decided to take the children, in her place, for the annual acorn gathering. Things went badly for them, as you well know, and had it not been for the three of you…well, lets not think of that."

"I'm so proud of you and at the Winter Ball I shall speak of your deeds to all of Sharrock. You will be given a special honor," the Queen said smiling. "But for now, it would be my pleasure to have you join me for breakfast."

The two girls let out a quiet little squeal of excitement and they followed the Queen to the huge dining room.

Gidley almost choked and suddenly breakfast didn't seem like a very good idea. He followed the girls, but he was sure he couldn't eat a thing and he wasn't at all sure he could handle the tools that he had heard the Queen used for dining. Gidley, like most of the common Elves, usually used a small knife for cutting up the food and he ate with his fingers. 'Oh, no' he thought, 'how can I get through this?'

The dining room was the largest room, other than the throne room, that the friends had ever seen. The table alone could not fit into any of their whole houses. It was set with elegant plates and glasses and eating tools. Fresh flowers were everywhere. If this is breakfast, what must the other meals be like?

There were fruits and berries and nuts and vita. Gidley took a quick sip of his vita, to calm himself down. The two girls were staring wide-eyed, but didn't seem nervous. Excited, but definitely not as scared as he was.

The pots of golden honey sparkled in the morning sun, coming through the stained glass windows and those same windows cast lovely colors over the pots of cream. Scones were piled high on a platter. They were dazzled by the food. Elves are not meat eaters and even though most of what the Queen had to eat was the same foods they all usually ate, they had never had all of them at once and never of such quantity or quality.

Casha and Bellina decided not to waste a moment and began to eat immediately. Gidley decided he'd better try to eat something.

Surprisingly, he found that the vita did calm him and when he started to eat, he found he did, indeed, have his appetite back.

They savored every bite!

When breakfast was over the Queen bade them farewell, with her thanks, and they left the palace full and happier than they ever remembered.

"I'm overwhelmed," exclaimed Casha.

Bellina nodded agreement, a big smile on her face.

As they walked along Gidley realized that it was the quietest it had ever been with the girls around. He started to make a smart remark, but changed his mind. They were all awestruck by the morning's happenings and he didn't want to spoil it for them. He just looked at them both and smiled and nodded.

Later that day, they all met in the middle of town to shop and talk about the exciting and incredible last two days. Everything had finally started to sink in.

"Do you believe we had *breakfast, with the Queen?*" Bellina asked. You could tell by the way she said it, that she surely didn't believe it herself.

"What do you suppose will happen at the Winter Ball? Do you think she meant we were to actually go there ourselves?" Casha asked.

"It sounded to me like she was just going to make an announcement to the town, before the Winter Ball started. We did save a war hero. I guess we should be proud of ourselves," Gidley answered.

"We should be proud anyway. We saw someone needed us and we helped. I don't think it matters if he's a war hero or not," Casha said.

"No, I didn't mean it that way," Gidley said. "We saw a need and responded. I'm proud of us for being brave long enough to help."

Chapter 3

SNOW HOLIDAY

The first snow was always magical. It covered all the rough, bare places with sparkly, cold snowflakes that looked just like the crystals that came from the mines, all crushed up and spread everywhere. It signaled that winter had arrived.

Every year, in all of Sharrock, there was excitement when the first snow of the year had fallen. That was because it meant a holiday for all the hard working Elves.

They had harvested crops and dried and stored food for the winter and had filled barrels with water and made enough vita for all of their families to drink and stay warm and healthy all winter. And they had made stables for their ponies, in barns warm and dry and stocked with plenty of food. And they made sure their own homes were safe and warm and dry. Then they needed a rest and tradition was, that they kept very busy until the first snow. That first snow signified the end of labor and to celebrate the Elves threw a huge party, on that night. But this year the snow was very late. Everyone wondered when it would come.

As soon as the Elves awoke this morning and saw that the first snow had fallen overnight, there was much joy. There was no work today, except for the preparation of food and drink for the night's party, and most Elves didn't think of *that* as work at all. Everyone pitched in to help and they laughed and joked all day.

Their party was very special to them, so they would get out their best clothes and their flutes and fiddles and dance and eat until dawn.

Even the Fairies from Kellenshire would come to say thanks for all the help given to them and they would bring magical things that only Fairies knew how to make.

Just before noontime, they all ran to their windows to find out what all the noise was about outside on the street. All were surprised to see the Queen's guards going door to door and announcing that the Queen wanted them all in the palace courtyard at six-o'clock that evening.

Everyone came outside and began talking and speculating with their neighbors, about the strange request. Elves all across Sharrock were invited to the palace and they all wanted to know why.

Every year the Queen had a special Winter Ball at the palace on this night. All the royal friends and families from the surrounding shires and realms were invited. This was a much grander party than the one the common Elves had, both in food and dress, with more elaborate decorations. So why have everyone come to the palace tonight?

"Gidley, do you think that's what Queen Findra meant that day? You know, the day we had breakfast with her?" Casha asked.

"Oh, about us being spoken of? I guess so. What else could she have meant?"

"I kind of thought maybe she meant exactly what she's doing. She's having everyone come to the courtyard and maybe she is going to thank us publicly," Casha said. "And I think we had better go find Bellina and see what we should do"

"Do about what?" Gidley wanted to know.

"Clothes, silly. Fine garb. Bellina and I need to prepare what we will wear if the Queen has us up on the balcony. We need something grand," Casha explained, as she started walking towards Bellina's house. Turning, she asked, "Aren't you coming Gidley?"

"Ah, I don't have anything grand to wear," Gidley called to her. "Besides I don't think the Queen meant for us to *actually be seen*. I think it's just a formality." He realized that Casha was walking very fast and was out of hearing range.

With a sigh of resignation, Gidley followed, more confused and nervous than he had ever been in his life. Could the Queen really want to have *them,* on the balcony with her? Just thinking of it made his head reel.

He caught up with Casha and they both arrived at Bellina's house together. They found her running around her house, frantically pulling clothes out of every drawer. She rushed to her friends and started sputtering about the Winter Ball and honors and clothes.

"Whoa, whoa, whoa!" Casha told her friend. "Stop and just get a hold of yourself. I can't understand a word you're saying."

"The Queen, she, the ball, we, oh what will we wear? I'm so, I'm so… oh, Casha, Gidley. We aren't…we don't have…oh, oh." Bellina sputtered to a halt.

"Hey, calm down," Gidley said. "I'm getting a headache." He ran to the cupboard and grabbed a wooden bowl and a jar of vita. He brought it to Bellina. "Drink this, please," he begged.

Bellina took a large swallow of vita and immediately calmed down.

"I'm sorry, and thank you, Gidley," she sobbed. "I got so flustered when I heard the news about the Winter Ball and I panicked. We have no fine clothes to wear. We'll look like fools at that Ball!"

"Bellina, stop." Casha held her friend. "We need to wear the best clothes we have because we may…*may,* get to go up, on the balcony, because the Queen *may,* say a few words in public about our heroic deeds. We aren't going to the Winter Ball. Why ever would you get such a crazy idea as that?"

"Oh, you don't understand," Bellina wailed. "My cousin, Litta, stopped by about an hour ago. She told me that she heard that three special heroes were being honored at the Winter Ball, tonight! She knows things like that, because she works in the palace kitchen. She said all the other kitchen Elves are talking about it.

"Oh, my," Casha said, sitting all the way down to the floor.

Gidley rushed over. Casha was pale and gratefully took and gulped down the jar of vita that he handed her. He, himself, took a large swig directly from the storage vessel.

Bellina giggled, "Aren't we a fine group of heroes. Quaking in our shoes over a party!"

They all laughed.

Gidley put it all into perspective when he said, "The Queen may be giving us a special honor, but she also knows that we don't have fine clothes. She only expects us to dress in the best we have."

At that moment, there was a knock at the door. Bellina, still laughing, ran to open it. There stood the guard, whom they remembered from that wonderful morning of the breakfast.

"Miss Bellina, I...oh, Miss Casha and Master Gidley, there you are. Pardon me, but we have been searching for you two. We should have known you would have already heard the news and would be together." The guard continued, "Her Majesty, has sent me to invite you all to the Winter Ball this evening. She has sent her seamstresses and her tailors to adjust your finery for this evenings festivities." With that, he stepped aside and three young ladies and two young men entered, carrying sewing baskets, clothes and shoes.

"I shall leave you to get your dress prepared," the guard told them. I shall return for you at five-thirty, to escort you to the palace. Will you be here or at your own homes?"

"Here!" all three friends said at once. "Thank you," they all said together again.

When the guard had gone, all three rushed together and locked arms and danced around singing, "Going to the Ball, going to the Ball".

Gidley remembered the visitors and turning red in the face, halted their dance. "Uh, I think we need to be fitted for clothes."

Chapter 4

SOMETHING MISSING

At precisely five-thirty that evening the three friends heard the sound of ponies approaching Bellina's house. Running to the window, all three caught their breath. Coming down the street was a fine carriage pulled by four, white ponies.

Not only were Casha, Bellina and Gidley dressed in the most splendid clothes they had ever worn, now, they would get their first ever carriage ride.

Casha was the most beautiful that Gidley had ever seen her. Dressed in pale lavender, her eyes were more violet than ever. Her hair was pulled back with ribbons and berry juice stained her lips pink.

"If I die right now, I will have died seeing the most perfect thing in the world." Gidley hoped he hadn't said that out loud, but seeing Casha blush, he thought maybe he had. He grinned at her.

Bellina was a vision herself, in pale blue. She had small, white flowers in her hair, which tonight she chose to leave long and straight and she wore a gold locket, that had belonged to her mother, around her neck. Surely they were the most gorgeous Elves, in all the world. Gidley sighed. He was so proud to be seen with them.

Not that every girl who saw Gidley that night wouldn't be dreaming of him for many months and very jealous of Casha and Bellina. He was handsome, in black tights and black shirt, with a golden embroidered jerkin, belted with real leather. The knee high black boots lent him a dashing air.

Just at that moment, there came a knock at the door. The carriage had arrived at Bellina's door. "Ladies, shall we go to the ball?" Gidley said, offering each girl an arm.

They were whisked off, the ponies doing a swift trot. In minutes they had arrived at the gates of the palace. The gates opened and the carriage entered the courtyard and drew up in front of the door.

The friends were helped down from the carriage and escorted through the door.

All three drew in gasping breaths, as they saw how extraordinary the palace looked when dressed for the Winter Ball. The Fairies must have used up all their Fairy Dust. Everything sparkled. And, where did all the roses come from? It was the start of winter season. No roses bloomed now.

"Please come to the ballroom," the guard urged. The Queen awaits you."

Too awestruck to be nervous, all three followed the guard. What they saw in the ballroom nearly made their hearts stop. *Beautiful* was not a word good enough to describe *this room*. There must have been every candle and crystal in the world, and all the food. It was too magnificent to comprehend.

"Welcome," the Queen said, as she arose from her chair. She was breathtaking, in a dark purple gown that was far too beautiful for Casha or Bellina, to ever imagine wearing. Her amethyst jewels sparkled purple, in the candlelight.

"We must go upstairs to the balcony. I need to make an announcement to my subjects. Come quickly."

The three friends tried to bow and follow, at the same time.

Outside throngs of Eves and Fairies began to gather under the balcony. They had never been summoned like this before. They waited and wondered. Some knew, of course, for rumors were running throughout Sharrock about the young heroes.

At that moment, the Queen and her court stepped onto the balcony and everyone bowed down.

"Arise, my subjects and listen to me," the Queen began and there was a muffled sound, as all rose to hear her.

"As many of you may have heard," the Queen continued, "we have here in Sharrock, three, fine, brave, young Elves. At danger to themselves, they defended and rescued Atilol, one of our finest heroes, and his two grandchildren. With Atilol's blessings and thanks and, with my own pride at having such brave and wonderful subjects, I present to you, Gidley, Casha and Bellina. Heroes of the Queen's Court."

Deafening applause broke out as the guards pushed the three, suddenly shy, heroes forward. Everyone was proud of them and as they were most popular, among the Elves of Sharrock, no one felt jealous or had evil thoughts over their good fortune tonight.

The Queen stepped forward, "Gidley, you first responded to the call for help and you killed the lupode, that threatened Atilol and the children. And with help from your friends, removed a branch pinning Atilol to the ground. You ran swiftly to Sharrocktown and brought back help. Atilol, our greatest hero, is still alive because of you, our newest hero. Atilol came to the palace several weeks ago and returned this to me." A guard stepped forward holding a dagger. "This is *The Dagger of Bahyel*. It is given to the one who performs the bravest deed. We haven't given it to anyone since it was presented to Atilol after the war, many years ago. He earned it by saving the life of my Father, King Bowdin. We have very little trouble here and no cause to have heroes. We have many kind deeds, but very little need of brave ones. I present this to you, for your bravery."

The applause thundered up to the balcony. Gidley, shaking and dry mouthed, saw himself reach out his hand and grasp the dagger. All he could do was smile and hold the dagger aloft, for all to see.

"Bellina and Casha," said the Queen, "you both ran to help Gidley, with little thought for your own danger. You helped Gidley remove the limb from Atilol's body and stayed with the children, until more help arrived. To keep them calm, Bellina, you played your flute and Casha, you sang to them. While there is only one Dagger, I feel I must honor you both for your parts in that brave day."

"To Bellina, I present the magical Flute that once belonged to my Father, King Bowdin. You will now have powerful magic, in the music you produce. Don't misuse it," the Queen said, handing her a golden flute.

Bellina took the flute, with shaking hands and tears fell down her cheeks. This was much more than she ever would have dreamed of.

"To Casha, I bestow the gift of reason and voice. Your words will always come to your aid. Speak carefully. This gold ring isn't magical, but I want you to have it. It was a gift to me, from my father. I know he would be pleased, for you to wear it."

"Thank you, I shall treasure this all my life," was all Casha could say. No words came to her aid, this time.

"Now, I must make mention of the Elves who came back with you Gidley, and returned Atilol and the children to safety in town. They are three friends of yours and I thank you all. I shall order a small income for the six of you. It will be paid annually and will be enough to keep you all well fed and housed for the rest of your lives."

A roar of h*ero, hero, hero,* arose, from the crowd.

"Quiet, please!" said Queen Findra. "I know you all are anxious to begin your celebration of winter. Go home and get your food and flutes and return here. It is a pleasant night. You will hold your party here, in the courtyard. I know you will want to congratulate our fine heroes."

The Queen turned and started down to the ballroom. Casha, Gidley and Bellina followed her and the royal court.

The party was grand. They danced and ate and sang and danced some more! They met many royals and distinguished guests, from the surrounding Realms of Kellenshire, Sanadula and Vallard. The three friends would look at each other and burst out in giggles and hug and giggle some more. Even Gidley danced tonight.

They all stepped outside to the courtyard from time to time and received congratulations and hugs from everyone.

At close to ten o'clock, three strangers approached Gidley, who was sitting alone outside, taking a little cool air and resting.

"Well, well, the little hero," said the first Elf, who introduced himself as Zirba. "These are my friends, Bomid and Losard."

"Hello," Gidley said. "Nice to meet you. I don't recall having seen you before."

"You haven't. We come from another kingdom. Your Queen sent out invitations, to royalty and friends, all across the land," Losard said.

"We had no idea that she would have this special presentation to you and your little girlfriends," added Zirba.

"Pretty little things," sneered Losard.

They had dark hair and shifty eyes and they all looked alike to Gidley, except for the one called Zirba, who had a beard. He thought they were all probably older than he was and they looked big and menacing. Gidley began to feel very nervous.

Presentation on the balcony

'Boy, if Queen Findra only knew what a coward, I really am,' thought Gidley.

The three laughed and slapped him on the back and he started to relax a little. They may have had a little too much wine, but they probably weren't dangerous.

"We'd like to have a close look at your dagger," Zirba announced. "I've

21

heard of it, but never thought I'd ever get a chance to actually see it. Won't we have a tale, for the Dords?"

"I guess I could show you," Gidley reluctantly said, and he pulled the dagger from the sheath.

It gleamed in the moonlight and from the candlelight spilling through the window. The blade was forged of the finest steel, which made a beautiful swirl pattern, honed to a fine point. The hilt was of inlaid gold, encrusted with diamonds and a yellow stone, which formed a dragon wrapped around the handle. One enormous ruby was set, just above the blade and an emerald topped the hilt. Even the sheath was covered in gemstones. Gidley had just gotten his first good look at it, and he could hardly breathe. All three strangers reached for it at the same time and Gidley reflexively pulled it back with a gasp.

They laughed and said they only wanted to look at it, not steal it. Gidley felt foolish for jerking it away from them and held it out so they could see it up close. The looks that came over their faces made him feel uneasy again, but they didn't do anything except look.

Gidley put it back in its sheath, as quickly as he could without seeming too anxious.

"Those gems are priceless, you know," Zirba said. "It has the last known examples of the gem, kimbar. They're the little yellow ones that form the dragon on the hilt. I understand your dagger was made years ago, by a wizard, and I hear there's a spell cast on it. It was used by the King himself during the war. He's the one who personally gave it to Atilol, for saving his life."

"I, I don't know about any of that," Gidley stammered. He had no idea that he possessed such a wonderful and fine thing. "Thanks for the information."

"Hey, no problem," Bromid said. "We'll see you around. Here have a drink on me."

Gidley breathed a sigh of relief when they had gone, and he took a big gulp of the drink before he realized that it was wine. He had never had wine before, but it was good and cool. He finished it and after a few minutes went inside to find Casha and Bellina and dance some more.

After looking around the crowded ballroom for several minutes, he spotted Casha and Bellina, off to the side sitting and laughing. They were surrounded by several handsome, young Elves.

"Oops! Looks like I'd better get over there, before Casha forgets who I am," Gidley laughed.

"Where have you been?" Casha jumped up and demanded.

The young Elves looked at each other and backed away from Casha and Bellina.

"I went out to get some fresh air," Gidley said, somewhat embarrassed.

"Fresh air?" Casha asked. "Fresh air for *three hours?*" She brought her foot down on the last two words, for emphasis. "We looked all over for you."

"Three hours?" a startled Gidley asked. "Oh no, I was only gone a few minutes. I met some foreign guests and we talked a short while, but I only went out, at ten o'clock."

"It's almost one-thirty," Bellina informed him.

Gidley blinked a few times, "One-thirty? Are you serious?"

"Where were you?" Casha asked again.

"I told you. I talked to some guests who wanted to see my dagger," Gidley said looking down. His heart stopped.

The Dagger of Bahyel and its sheath, were gone!

Chapter 5

PROVISIONS AND PLANS

❧

"Where's your dagger?" screamed Casha, who had looked down, just at the same time Gidley did.

A sudden silence fell over the ballroom. It seemed that everyone had heard Casha. They all stood in shocked silence. Then, as if parted by a magic hand, the crowd formed a long path, through which Queen Findra walked.

"Where *is* your dagger?" the Queen asked, echoing Casha.

Gidley felt the room begin to swirl, but blinked and got hold of himself. "I don't know, Your Majesty. I was talking to some foreign Elves, at ten o'clock, and now it's one-thirty and I have no dagger."

"You don't have any memory of the past three and a half hours?" the Queen demanded.

"No, ma'am." Gidley swallowed hard trying not to cry. "I thought it was still around ten o'clock. I don't know what happened."

"Something must have happened. That is very obvious. Who were the foreign Elves you speak of? Did they give you drugs that would have knocked you out? Speak up," Queen Findra yelled.

"I showed them the dagger and they told me a little of the history of it, but I still had it when they left. I didn't eat or …oh," Gidley stopped.

"Or what?" the Queen demanded.

"One of them, Bomar, I think his name was, gave me the rest of his wine. I never had wine before. I guess I drank it before I realized, what I was doing. They made me nervous looking at the dagger, you know?"

"What I *know* is that you have lost *The Dagger of Bahyel* and I *know*, that you had better have a little more bravery left in you, because I charge you to go after these thieves and bring the dagger back!"

Everyone stood in stunned silence. Gidley hoped a hole would open up in the floor, and that he would fall through. Or else wake up from, what he hoped, was surely a bad dream.

Casha and Bellina rushed over to him.

"Don't worry, Gidley," Casha said. "We'll go together and get that dagger back."

"Come on," said Bellina. "Lets go home."

The following morning Gidley was awakened by the Queen's guard knocking on his door.

"Master Gidley, you are to report to the Queen your plans for getting the dagger back. Round up your provisions and be at the palace, as soon as, you can.

All the horror of last night came rushing back to Gidley and he felt so sick he almost fell down. To be so honored one minute, and having such fun, and the next to have plunged into such a nightmare was almost more than Gidley could bear.

'Why did this happen? Was I negligent?' These questions ran through Gidley's mind. 'No,' he decided. 'I did save Atilol but I did not ask for the dagger. I did not ask for the honors, and I did not invite those evil Elves to the Winter Ball. Why would the Queen turn on me, so quickly?'

"Because, you lost the precious dagger, you idiot," Gidley chided himself. He dressed quickly and rushed over to Casha's house. He hoped his friends weren't too ashamed to see him. He needed them more than at any other time in his life, with the exception of the time his parents were killed.

"Casha will know what to do."

They sat around Casha's table and made plans. After Gidley had arrived that morning, Bellina came in a short while later. Gidley told them about his visit from the Queen's guard and the message that he had delivered to Gidley.

"It's simple," said Casha. "We go get it back."

"It's not so simple," Gidley almost cried. "We don't know where they came from, who they are or where they went. How do you find a small dagger, in this big world?"

"Well, first we ask the Queen for their names and where they are from. She invited them, she must know who they are. They certainly weren't from Sharrock. Also, we didn't ask for this. Queen Findra may be mad, but she must help us."

"Casha," Gidley began, "the Queen won't help us. How do you know she knows those thieves? And just what do you mean by help *us*? You don't think I'd drag you and Bellina into this mess, do you?"

"*Drag* us?" Casha asked. "I think we were all honored last night and I think if Queen Findra was so worried about that stupid dagger, she should have kept it for herself."

Bellina and Gidley's mouths dropped open. No one spoke of the Queen like that.

"Don't look at me like that you two. You know I'm right. Queen Findra can make us go get that dagger back, but she can't shame Gidley for something he had no control over. Those evil Elves were after that dagger, and who knows what they might have done to get it. We're just lucky Gidley didn't get hurt."

"That's right," Bellina added. "It's not Gidley's fault. Lets go see Her Majesty."

Of course, the girls lost their bravado, once they were face to face with the Queen. They could be mad and indignant at home, but here in the palace, it was a different story.

"Well, I see you brought your back-up team, Mr. Gidley. What are your plans for getting the dagger back?" the Queen demanded.

"Your Majesty. I'm so sorry for what happened. I feel like a complete fool. My friends have joined me for moral support, but I have no intention of endangering them by letting them go on my quest. I will do whatever it takes to get that dagger back. Please, forgive me."

"Look," the Queen snapped, then taking a deep breath, she said, in a kinder voice, "I was stunned to realize *The Dagger of Bahyel* had been stolen. I'm afraid I overreacted and blamed you. It's quite obvious, *you* were a victim. The dagger is priceless, however, and very dangerous, in the wrong hands. You must get it back. It was given to you, so, as the owner, *you* must claim it again. I certainly don't expect these two girls to go on such a dangerous quest, but I do not expect you to go alone. You must choose your team and leave at once. Oh, by the way, I know that you have no family in Sharrock to help you get provisions together. I'm prepared to supply you with food and clothes. I'll have someone bring them by, later. Now, please go!"

"Wait just a minute, Your Majesty," Casha interrupted. "Please, Bellina and I will go with Gidley. He is our dearest friend and we aren't just *any girls*. We happen to be the other two heroes honored, at last night's ball. We have the magic powers that you, yourself, bestowed upon us and we will be needed. We will go with him!"

"Don't ever talk back to me like that again, young lady! But, you are absolutely correct. You two must help young Gidley. I would be mad at you for speaking to me, as you just did, but I gave you the power of reasoning and what you say is reasonable. Now, please leave me."

The three bowed and hurried outside. In the courtyard, Bellina gave a whoop.

"You are so brave, Casha. The Queen could have had you killed for talking to her, like that."

"I don't care," Casha said. "She shouldn't treat Gidley so badly and dismiss us as, *two girls*. We were all heroes last night and today she speaks of us like we mean nothing."

"Come on, Gidley said," Let's get something to eat and get our stuff packed. We'll leave in the morning.

While the three friends were getting the last of their belongings together, there was a knock at the door.

When Gidley opened the door, he was surprised to see Dira standing there and behind him, Jinto and Reyal. They were the friends, who had helped that day in the woods. They were all good friends with Gidley, who had lived with Dira's family, after his own parents had been killed. Dira, at just three feet, seven inches tall, was the same height as Casha, but he out weighted her by forty pounds. He had black hair and blue eyes and while he couldn't be called handsome, he wasn't bad looking. A farmer, by trade, he lived with his mother and father and younger sister, not far from where Gidley lived now.

Reyal was taller, at four feet, and quite good-looking. He had light brown hair and soft brown eyes. When he smiled, everyone liked him right away and after talking to him a while, everyone liked him even better. He and his brother, Levat were the best carpenters in Sharrock. They lived in a small cottage, behind the home his parents shared with their youngest brother, Pard.

Jinto was the tallest of them all, just over four feet, and he had large arms and a barrel chest, which made him appear much larger. With his pale blond hair and light blue eyes, he had a kindly look about him. He had built up his muscles, by lifting the large stones he used to build walls and chimneys or anything else, he, as a stonemason, was called on to do. His family had been killed ten years before, so Jinto lived alone, in the small, stone, cottage, that his father had built.

"We're coming with you," said Dira.

"Yeah," added Reyal. "We aren't the heroes you three are, but we're the ones who brought the old Elf and the grandkids back from the woods."

"We feel like we was part of the rescue, like," Jinto said, stepping up next to Dira.

"Come in please," said Gidley. "I appreciate your concern and your offer of help, but I really can't endanger your lives."

"Oh, mister big, are ya?" Dira asked.

"We was good enough to help, remember?" Jinto asked.

"We are coming!" stated Reyal. "I believe the Queen mentioned our part in the rescue, too."

"Well, okay," Gidley looked at Casha and Bellina for help.

"Yes, of course they'll come," Casha stated. "We're going to need help, Gidley. You needn't feel guilty. You didn't ask them, they volunteered."

"We are embarrassed that you needed help at the party and we were having too much fun to notice those guys bothering you," Reyal added. "They stole your dagger and not one of us saw it."

Gidley assured them, that it was not up to them to mind him last night. He thanked them for being good friends and offering to come with him to retrieve the lost dagger.

And for several more hours, they formed the beginning of a plan to get back the dagger. All they had to go on was the information that Dira got from a young Elf who remembered seeing some strangers leave the party late last night, heading north. She heard them mention Vallard, a shire about two days travel, north of Sharrock.

Gidley and friends start their journey

Chapter 6

THE SEARCH BEGINS

Bright and early the next morning the party set out on their quest for the missing dagger.

The Queen's guard had come by late last night with bundles of food, a flask of Special Vita, and some cloaks made from Fairy silk for Casha, Gidley and Bellina, as she didn't know, at that time, that the other three had joined the party. The Queen had sent several Fairy silk blankets, however, so they each had at least one and there was one extra.

They each packed their bundles with wool socks, wool shirts and extra woolen pants. Even Casha and Bellina would wear pants, on this trip. Each had a woolen hat to be pulled low, over their large, pointed ears. Elves fear the cold on these delicate points and although the cold was often painful, no one in this group had yet lose a tip to the cold. They would all wear the heavy leather boots that were always worn, in winter, and they brought along their gloves.

Casha grabbed a large clean, soft, cloth and stuffed it in her bundle. Being practical, she knew it would make a good bandage, if one became necessary.

They all had made up bundles of food, which consisted of dried fruits and scones. Bellina had made a special recipe that she got, from her neighbor. It was a flat, bread, very crisp and sweet. When broken up and wrapped in cloth it remained fresh for over a week. It was good for a quick snack while walking and Bellina had made enough for each to have some in their bundles. And, of course, they all had vita.

They packed the extra bundles onto Jinto's pony. Dira and Reyal had families who would need their ponies and they all agreed it would be best to take just the one pony. Ponies were scarce in that part of the world. That also meant there would be less food and water that they would need to carry for extra ponies and that meant less to worry about. Jinto's pony would come in handy, however, if anyone got too tired and needed to ride.

Jinto had a couple of bundles filled with oats for his pony and he took the extra Fairy silk blanket to keep him warm. Jinto was a simple Elf, but very kind. He always thought of others first and he loved animals.

Bellina had the magic flute and even though she didn't know just what it did, she brought it along anyway. They all had their daggers and small knives for cutting up their food. Reyal brought his flute, also, and though it wasn't a magic flute he could play a sweet tune, nonetheless.

Atilol's daughter showed up just before they left and gave them three more cloaks. They were brown and very soft, and also woven from Fairy silk. The adventurers knew they would be warm now. At first, they each had selected a heavy woolen cloak to throw on over everything else, but now with enough of the lighter weight and much warmer Fairy silk cloaks to go around they all left the bulky, wool ones behind.

As they walked through Sharrocktown, many Elves came out of their homes and shouted 'goodbye' and 'good luck' and many other well wishes. A few of them handed the travelers bundles that contained more food and, in one case, quite a large bundle of crystals which they never thought about bringing themselves, but would need to purchase additional food and lodging along the way.

Bellina took out her flute and played softly, as they walked. Suddenly, they all felt peaceful and walking became easier.

At noon, after having covered quite a good distance, they all stopped just before crossing the Nork River and had their lunch.

"I asked around about them guys," Jinto said. "Nobody knows who they was."

"There were five altogether, I know that much," Dira said.

"Five!" shouted Gidley. "How do you know?"

"I thought I told you," Dira said. "That girl, Malla, saw the three guys talking to you and she thought one of them was kind of cute, so she followed them out of the courtyard. There were two more out there and they all rode off north, towards Vallard."

"This is just great," wailed Gidley. "We are off looking for a priceless dagger. None of us has a clue where we are going or whom we are going after. I just find out we are going after five Elves, not three. Great!"

"We will just have to keep each other informed," Casha added. "We can't assume someone knows something. We have to have a meeting everyday, to fill in the others. We may have to split up to cover more ground, when we get to the next town, and it will be even more important than ever that we all share information."

"Gidley, do you remember any of their names, yet?" asked Bellina.

"No. I think they put something in that wine. I do remember one was Bomur or something and I think I remember Zerta. I don't know. I've tried to remember, but I can't be positive."

After lunch, they looked at a map that Reyal had borrowed from his brother and found that the next town was located at the outer edge of Sharrock. Soon they would venture into other lands and they all felt afraid, although no one said it aloud.

After a suitable rest, they packed up the food and after replacing the water that they had used, were ready to continue to the next stop, which they now knew was the town of Neer.

Gidley was thinking just how far away, Neer, actually was. He tried to be brave, but he couldn't help but think what a nervous, scared, little Elf he really was. Casha and Bellina were doing better than he was. None of the three had ever been out of Sharrock, which was the realm of the Eves of their kingdom. He didn't know if Jinto, Dira or Reyal had ever been farther. They were older, so maybe they had been other places. No one had mentioned it, if they had.

'Just hope we make it, without anyone getting hurt,' he thought.

"Don't worry, Gidley. We'll be fine," Casha said.

"I guess I said that out loud, again. I'd better watch it."

Gidley needn't have worried, at least not yet, anyway. They made good time and were getting closer to Neer, where they planned to eat and rest. After walking about another hour, the group was singing and talking and really getting into this adventure thing. They were entering the Galta Forest, which began in Sharrock and continued into Vallard.

Unfortunately, Gidley, who was in the lead, and had really keen hearing, heard something. Stopping the group he turned to them.

"Please stop talking. I need to listen," Gidley pleaded.

"What?" asked Bellina. "Did you hear something?"

"What do you think you heard?" Casha asked. "Was it voices or just sounds?"

"Oh, don't ask a million questions. I heard something and it could be dangerous. Please, don't talk," Gidley begged.

"You're the one talking," Casha added.

"Uh, oh!" Jinto said.

"Run!" Dira yelled.

Lupodes

Chapter 7

THE ENCOUNTER

Lupodes! Five lupodes were running right towards them. They were big and gray with red eyes and huge teeth. They looked like wolves, but were larger and had long fur and big, rounded ears.

"Run," screamed Bellina.

"Climb a tree," yelled Gidley.

Everyone ran for the nearest tree. Jinto tried to jump to grab the lowest branch and missed several times. By the time he got a hold of the branch, a lupode was right beneath him. Straining and covered in sweat, Jinto pulled himself up and climbed, as fast, and as high, as he could. His startled pony had run back the way they had just come.

Dira had an easy time. The lupodes weren't even close to him, when he started his climb. He sat on the branch and peered down between the twigs.

Gidley and Bellina ran for the same tree, and Gidley gave her a push up and she reached down and helped him pull himself up.

Reyal couldn't find a tree with a limb low enough to climb and he was frantically looking around, when the first lupode reached him.

Reyal felt the jaws clamp down on his leg as he kicked and screamed in pain.

Suddenly, the lupode let go. Reyal, shaking and almost in tears turned to see Casha stabbing the lupode, with her dagger.

Immediately everyone else safe in the trees was overcome with shame. As they cowered in the trees, Casha was trying to save Reyal.

They all jumped down and pulled their daggers.

Gidley, who had experience killing lupodes, soon made short work of killing the one which had come running over towards him.

Bellina held her dagger in front of her and charged a lupode, with a murderous scream. Jinto, however, reached out and slashed down with his dagger wounding the animal. Then Jinto and Bellina stepped forward and both stabbed the lupode. Pulling their daggers free, they nodded to each other and turned to go after another lupode.

One of the terrible creatures had run over to Casha, just as she finished killing the lupode that was attacking Reyal, and she turned to defend herself.

With it snarling and snapping at her, Casha felt afraid, but she was also mad. How dare these things come here to hurt the kindly Elves of Sharrock. First Atilol and his grandchildren were threatened and now themselves. She pulled back her fist and let the vicious lupode have a hard hit right, on the end of his nose. He yelped and ran away into the trees.

Casha turned to do battle again, but three of the lupodes were dead and the other one had also run away.

The group, sitting down and breathing heavily, could only look at each other. No words would come for several minutes.

Bellina was the first to speak. "We need to tend to Reyal."

"I'm okay," Reyal said. "It's just a little bite."

"You'd better have some vita," Casha said, and handed a flask over to Reyal.

"Can you walk?" Dira wanted to know.

"Let me have some vita, first and then I'll try to walk," Reyal said.

After taking a long swig he tried to stand. It took him a few minutes to get up and put weight on his leg. He winced, but managed to take a few steps.

"I'm okay, I guess."

"You're still bleeding," Casha added. "We should look for a selim bush. The sap, when the bark is peeled, will stop the blood and then we can clean his leg and bandage it."

"Okay, everyone, Casha is right. Reyal can't keep bleeding. Does everyone know what a selim bush looks like?" asked Gidley.

Murmurs of 'yes', 'of course' and something Gidley wasn't sure he wanted to know, came from the group as they spread out to look for the remedy their friend needed.

They had searched for some time and Gidley was becoming upset that Reyal would bleed to death before they could find the one plant, that they knew would stop more blood loss.

"I've found some!" Dira called and rushed back towards his friend with a handful of twigs, that he was peeling as he ran.

After the juice was put on the bites, Casha pulled the strip of cloth from her bundle and gave it to Dira. Dira washed the blood away and using strips of Casha's cloth, wrapped some of the bark right onto Reyal's' leg.

"You may ride on the pony," Gidley told him. Jinto had found the pony not far away and had led him back to the group.

"Oh, no," Reyal protested. "I'll not tire the pony, unless it becomes absolutely necessary."

"Okay, but if you are in pain, please ride," Gidley begged.

"If I reach the point where I become more of a burden than a help, then I'll ride," Reyal declared. "Just let me have one more sip of vita. I'll be fine."

"If everyone is ready, we should get going. Maybe there is a healer in Neer, if we can get there," Gidley told them.

"Maybe we should get some more selim twigs, just in case we have a need for them," Casha suggested.

"That's not a bad idea."

"Are they good, if they dry out?" Bellina asked.

"No," Dira answered. "But maybe if we soak them, in some water, they might still work."

"We'll try it," said Gidley. "It can't hurt to try. Dira knows where the bush is so it will only take a few minutes for him to go back and get more."

While they waited for Dira to return with the twigs, everyone was engaged in discussion about the lupodes attack.

Casha noticed that Jinto was very quiet and she asked him what was wrong.

37

"It just be that I hate I had to kill that lupode, like, Miss Casha," he replied. "I know it be for saving our lives, still they must be hungry and driven to attack. They just be animals, like."

"Jinto I know you feel bad, now," Casha explained, "But sometimes it's necessary to defend yourself and your friends. We don't know what we may encounter as we go along. We may be called upon to do things we normally would never do."

"You be right, Miss," was all Jinto said.

"Jinto, my leg really hurts and I'm grateful that the animals were killed or driven off," Reyal told him. "Besides, would you rather have Casha or Bellina bitten, too?"

"Oh, no!" Jinto said, jumping up. "I'd not be wanting anyone hurt by them, like. I just hate, as they are mean enough to attack and we have to kill them."

Just then, Dira returned with some twigs and they packed them with a little water, that they hoped would keep them from drying out, in case it ever became necessary to use them.

"Oh," sighed Gidley, as they started off. "This is so hard."

Chapter 8

NEER, BUT NOT VERY FAR

It was getting late in the afternoon and the little band of weary Elves had finally reached Neer. Earlier, Bellina had played her flute to help their travels and Casha sang a little, but now they just trudged along in silence.

"My feet hurt," Casha whined.

"My whole body hurts," added Bellina.

"Well, yes, the whole body, but mainly the feet," Casha insisted.

"You two can't be complaining, already. Can you?" Gidley asked.

Both girls gave him a look that Gidley interpreted as 'keep quiet, you silly Elf!'

"I can tell you, *I'm* all in," Dira added.

"Yeah, me too, but mightn't we rest a bit and get Reyal looked after and see if we be finding them crooks?" asked Jinto. "Maybe not, in that order, but all them things, like?"

"Sure, Jinto, we'll do that." Gidley informed him. "However, I'm not sure what we should do. To see who we need, to find out the stuff we need to find out."

"Huh?" they all said at once.

"I mean, who we should see, to find out the stuff we need to know," Gidley tried again.

"There must be an Elf in charge, somewhere," Casha offered. "Let's ask someone."

The group left Reyal and the pony under a tree, near the edge of town and set out looking for someone who could point them in the direction they needed to go to find food and beds for the night, and help for their friend.

They were in luck and didn't need to ask anyone. Right there, not far inside the town they saw the sign for the 'Silver Bell Inn'.

Upon entering, Gidley went up to a rather tall, slim Elf dressed in brown pants and shirt, wearing a crisp white apron and asked if he were the proprietor.

"Why, yes, I am, sir," Murkle answered. "What can I do for you?"

"Well, we need some help," Gidley explained. "We're on a quest, ordered by Queen Findra and…"

"I know who you are," Murkle interrupted "I was at the celebration a few days ago. I'm sorry for your troubles, about that dagger. Bad stuff, that. I'll guess you need rooms and food?"

"Yes, thank you," Gidley said. "Also, we were attacked by lupodes a ways back and one of our traveling companions was bitten. Is there someone in town who could tend him?"

"Oh, there's been a lot of trouble with lupodes around here lately. No one knows why they are so far south. Lucky for your friend, my daughter is a healer. She has studied herbs and plants and will know what to do."

"Okay, great!" We'll go get Reyal and the pony," Dira said and motioned for Jinto to follow him.

Casha and Bellina were already sitting by the fire. It had been unseasonably warm since the first snowfall, a few days ago, and most of the snow had almost disappeared. However, since sundown, the temperature had really dropped and they had all become chilled. The fire felt very good.

"I can't believe we've walked this long and we still aren't out of Sharrock yet," Bellina sighed.

"I know. It's going to be a lot longer than I thought. I just hope we don't get bad weather," Gidley said.

"I hope we find those guys in a couple of days and get that dagger back, so we can go home," Casha stated.

Murkle came over, at that moment, and set down some pots of warm tea, just as Dira and Jinto came in with Reyal.

"I'll get my daughter," Murkle said and turned and went up the stairs.

He reappeared a few minutes later with a lovely Elf girl, whom he introduced with pride as his daughter, Amelli. She was about three feet, eleven inches tall, with brown hair that was wrapped around her head like a large, soft bun. Her eyes were the color of rich chocolate and she had a beautiful smile, with small white teeth. She went right to work on Reyal's leg. After cleaning it up, she made a rather smelly poultice of some kind of herbs and what appeared to be mud. Actually, it was mud.

Since he didn't appear to be in much pain and wasn't feverish, Amelli suggested he eat something, take a good draught of vita and get some sleep.

Everyone thanked her and she went back upstairs.

The friends surveyed the room. The main part of the Inn was made of stone, which Jinto commented on, as being 'very tight'. The fire was built in a good-sized fireplace and the orange glow made everything seem relaxed and comfortable.

They all ate and drank and let the fire warm out all the sore spots. It wasn't long before they had Murkle show them to their beds, for the night.

They all slept deeply and peacefully. Except Gidley, who tossed and turned for quite a while trying to figure out just what they might have to do to get the dagger back, if they ever were able to find the thieves.

The next morning dawned gray and overcast. The little group wasn't cheered by the weather, which had turned cold and snow flurries fell during breakfast.

Amelli checked Reyal's leg and put another poultice on it. She advised him to remain at the Inn and wait for his friends to return for him, or to go back to Sharrocktown.

Reyal insisted that he felt well enough to continue with his friends and reluctantly, Amelli agreed with him. She gave him some extra poultice ingredients, which she made him promise to put on his wounds, at least two more days.

After conferring over the map, the party found that they needed to get to the next shire, which was Woodglen.

Woodglen, Murkle informed them was a shire made up mostly of lumbermen.

"Woodglen, being made up mostly, of just trees," he said laughing.

"All woods! I hope we don't run into any more lupodes," Dira exclaimed.

They all agreed.

Gidley tried to settle the debt to Murkle for all the services he had provided, but Murkle refused the crystals, saying that he was honored to have the heroes stay with him.

"Atilol was my commander during the war and I would have done anything for him," Murkle assured them. "I'm glad you spared him to live a little longer."

Gidley insisted that he take a few crystals to give to Amelli, and Murkle said he would be happy to take a couple for her.

After saying their good byes and collecting the pony, the little group started off in what was becoming quite a snowstorm.

They arrived in the town of Oakleaf, very late that night. They were cold and tired, for they had walked a long way and the snow blew into their faces and chilled them. The walking was hard and Reyal was forced to ride on the pony, part of the way. That caused the others to be further burdened by the extra bundles they had to carry.

They had stopped briefly at noontime to eat, but they were so cold they decided they would rather be hungry and keep moving.

It was so boring, walking along. Woodglen was indeed made up of mostly trees, and all day the little group saw nothing but endless trees and a flat, colorless landscape covered in snow. Only the green needles of the pine, fir and spruce trees broke up the bleakness.

They all kept their eyes and ears open for lupodes, but fortunately none were seen or heard.

Bellina had been so miserable and cold and hungry, that she hadn't played her flute all day.

The warm beds they found at the small inn, at Oakleaf, were appreciated by all, that night.

Chapter 9

THE STORM

Bellina was the first up the next morning and she couldn't believe the snow that greeted her. She ran to Casha and woke her up.

"What?" Casha asked, jumping out of bed. "Is something wrong?"

"There's a heck of a lot of snow out there. It's going to really slow us down. Reyal will probably still have to ride the pony, so to make matters worse, we'll have more bundles to carry, again today," Bellina said.

But as it turned out, Reyal was much better and did end up walking the whole day. Amelli's poultices really worked.

Once everyone was up and had eaten breakfast, they settled their bill with the landlord. They had asked if anyone remembered seeing five Elves a few days before, but the landlord informed them that there were travelers through Woodglen all the time, as they supplied most of the lumber, for the area. No particular strangers would be noted.

Having dressed warmly, and wrapping themselves in the Fairies cloaks, they had started out on the day's journey. More of the same scenery as yesterday greeted them in a cold, unfriendly way.

The map said they should head to Vallard, which was a small, Elf Shire ruled over by a cousin of Queen Findra.

The biggest problem they faced was the Janego River, which they would have to cross in all the snow. No one looked forward to that.

Again today, as the snow fell at an alarming rate, the group decided to skip the stop for lunch. They ate a little food as they walked along. Pushing through the deepening snow was wearing them out and the cold made them thirsty.

"I'm having quite a tough time," Reyal informed them.

"I'm really sorry," Gidley offered. "But all I can say is 'get on the pony'."

"No, no, no. I really couldn't," Reyal said. "I just need to stop a while and rest. Not long enough for us to freeze to death, but I can't make another step."

They stopped for a few minutes and had a quick bite. After Reyal had a little vita, he felt a good deal better and they started off again.

Still, it was dusk as they finally got to the river. And what a cold and angry looking river it was!

Gidley gave a shudder as he stood looking across that dark, gray, forbidding barrier.

Jinto spotted the bridge that they were to cross. It was fairly new and kept in good repair by the Elves from Woodglen. It was made of wooden planks and was about five feet wide, with a rope tied to a pole at either end, as a handhold. It spanned the river, which appeared to be, about twenty-five or thirty feet across.

Normally five feet would be a comfortable width for crossing over on, but with the darkness and snow and the river swirling underneath, it was a recipe for disaster. The five-foot width shrunk to seem only about two feet wide.

They decided that Dira, Gidley and Reyal should go first to help clear the way, with Casha and Bellina going next, and Jinto and the pony going last.

It was hard to see where they were going and the rope handhold swayed in the strong wind. They all had a hard time holding on.

At about four feet from the bank, Bellina slipped and the next thing anyone knew she had fallen off the side of the bridge, into that awful, cold, gray water and worse, she had lunged forward and grabbed Dira and had taken him into the water with her!

Casha lunged for Bellina, as did Gidley and Reyal. Gidley and Reyal collided and because it was slippery and Reyal had a hard time standing

44

on his bad leg, they both went down. Gidley got one arm and one leg in the water, but managed to keep himself from going completely in.

Trouble at Janego River

Casha got a hold of Bellina and tried to pull her back onto the bridge. She wasn't strong enough, however, so Bellina just turned and struggled, with the current, towards the riverbank. After several tries and now shaking like a leaf from the cold, she managed to pull herself partway up the bank. Then she collapsed.

No one could see Dira and they all panicked.

Gidley had run to the end of the bridge first and pulled Bellina up onto the top of the riverbank. A few yards down stream, they heard Dira calling for help. He had managed to grab a small shrub that grew near the water and he held on for his life. Jinto rushed down and pulled his friend to safety.

"This is terrible," Gidley yelled. "Casha, what are we going to do?"

"Bellina and Dira have to get warm, as fast as they can and you and I are both about as wet. I don't know if Reyal and Jinto got wet. I think the pony was the only one spared," Casha said.

"How do we warm them?" Jinto asked.

"Don't we have a fire box?" asked Casha.

"We have a fire box, but what do we burn? Everything is covered with snow. This is terrible," Gidley yelled again.

"Gidley, don't panic," Casha warned. "Our friends will die, if we don't come up with a way to warm them quickly."

"I'm the only one not too wet," Jinto said. "It seems as it should be me, as gets some wood. There's branches and leaves and such under them trees."

"Good idea," Casha shouted. "Everyone. We must run and get under one of those evergreen trees, there. We'll have to change our clothes, as quickly as we can. It's dark so no one will see. We can build a fire and get close together."

They ran, as fast as they could manage with wet, heavy, wool clothes, through the falling snow. Casha and Gidley helped Bellina, who could hardly move by this time. Jinto picked Dira up and followed them. Reyal got the pony and made his way toward the tree.

A large fir tree yielded plenty of room underneath and offered more than enough wood to start a fire.

The low drooping branches formed a kind of roof and sides, so they were actually quite secure under there. The thick branches also stopped the wind. The many years of fallen needles made a deep, soft seat.

Gidley held up a cloak and Casha helped Bellina change clothes. Jinto did the same for Dira. Luckily, the cloaks made from the Fairies material, were dry immediately and they all wrapped up in them and pulled the blankets, from the bundles. They hung the wet clothes over some branches to dry.

Once the fire was going good, they got out some food and drank some vita and got close together, to share the warmth. It took a while, but eventually, everyone fell asleep.

At some point during the night, Jinto got the pony and moved him closer, under the tree.

Dira woke up and raised his head and looked at him.

"He was cold, like and alone," Jinto explained.

Dira, lay back down and went back to sleep.

Chapter 10

HELP COMES

The friends spent a cold restless night. In the morning Jinto built up the smoldering fire and everyone ate breakfast. It was snowing so hard and the wind blew so strong, that they all realized they probably weren't going anywhere for a while.

"We'd get lost, if we tried to find our way while this storm rages," Gidley cautioned. "It will stop soon, I'm sure."

Gidley was wrong, however, and the storm raged all day and all night.

By the following morning, Casha made a startling discovery. Some of the bundles of food were missing.

"Well, yes, I imagine so," said Gidley, when Casha mentioned it to him.

"I seen a couple get kicked off the bridge, like," Jinto added.

"So, we're low on food?" asked Bellina.

"That and we don't have much fire starter left, in the fire box," said Dira.

"Don't we have other fire boxes?" asked Gidley.

"Had some, don't no more," Jinto answered.

"Oh, this is just great," Gidley said, throwing both hands in the air.

"I was feeding the pony last night and checked the bundles," Jinto told them. "We got crystals and that Special Vita from the Queen, like."

"I'd like to save the Queen's Special Vita, for an emergency. No use using it unless we have to."

"I'd say we are reaching emergency," Casha said. "It's been two days and we haven't been able to move from here and we aren't getting any more food."

"We still got some food," Jinto announced. "I checked the bundles, like, and some, as what we got handed, as we was leaving, was, well… food."

"We still have to be careful," Gidley cautioned. "We may have, what seems like enough food now, but who knows how long we'll be here."

"Gidley's right," Dira put in. "No use using up all the food today and starving tomorrow."

"Well, is there any reason why we can't eat a little breakfast?" Bellina asked. "I'm so hungry."

"What about water?" asked Reyal.

"I'd think as you'd be remembering the river, there," said Jinto.

Everyone laughed.

The group spent most of the day snuggled under the tree. When Jinto got up to check on and feed the pony, Reyal asked him to get him his flute. Bellina thought that was a good idea and pulled hers from its holder, strapped around her waist. She thought how fortunate, that she hadn't lost the Queen's gift, when she fell into the river.

Reyal and Bellina played some of their favorite tunes and Casha even sang along with a few of them. They all cheered up immediately.

This must be the magic, Gidley thought.

When the two musicians started playing a spirited rendition of *Frolicking Elves*, everyone sang along and clapped in time.

When the song ended, Dira said, "I wish I had my fiddle. We could dance!"

They laughed and sang the last chorus again, louder than before.

As they ended, Gidley asked them to wait a minute, before starting a new tune.

"I thought I heard something," Gidley warned.

"Oh, no I hope it isn't a lupode, again! I couldn't take it," Bellina cried.

"Hello, hello," a voice called.

"Hello, to you," Gidley called back.

"Where are you?" asked the voice.

"We're here, under the tree," Gidley said, as he stuck his head out. "Where are you?"

"We're here. Oh, I see you," the voice called out again. "May we approach?"

"Sure, who are you?" Gidley asked.

"I'm Lorge and I'm with my friend Elb. Who are you?"

"Hello, I'm Gidley. I'm here with my friends Casha, Bellina, Jinto, Dira and Reyal. We are from Sharrocktown, in the Realm of Sharrock."

"What are you doing *here*?" Lorge asked, as he came closer, his pony snorting from the blowing snow. Dismounting, he walked over and peered under the branches. He was average height for an Elf, which was about three feet, ten inches, with longish, black hair and thick, black eyebrows that made him look like he was frowning. He wore a long, gray, woolen cloak wrapped around his thin body.

"We heard your music."

"Come in," Casha invited and they all moved over to make room.

Elb stuck his head in a few moments later, and then joined them. He was about the same height as his friend and extremely skinny. He, also, wore a woolen cloak and the friends almost laughed when he lowered the hood. He wore his brown hair cut so short it made his ears look larger than normal, even for an Elf, and they stuck out at an odd angle.

"We come from a town called Kudar, in Thorpeshire, northwest of here. We're heading to Woodglen to see some of Lorge's relatives. The weather wasn't bad when we left home, but it sure got bad quickly. We thought if we pushed on southward we might get out of this storm," Elb explained. "There's not a lot of snow, but it's extremely cold and that wind blows so hard, that it kicks up the snow and blows it right into your face. You can't see two feet ahead."

"We're heading north on business for Queen Findra," Gidley told them. "We had an accident on the bridge and lost our second fire box and some of our food. We've been under this tree for two days. It will be our third night."

"You're welcome to have some of our food," Lorge offered. "We can get more food in Woodglen. We hope to cross the river, when we leave here. Is the bridge alright, or was it part of your accident?"

"Some of us fell off and got wet and we lost some food, but the bridge was undamaged," Gidley said.

"We just be falling off, like. I don't know what happened during the storm. The wind is powerful, like," Jinto added.

'Well, there's a place about a mile down that we could cross, if we have to, but we would get wet, too. And a mile, in this storm is a long, long way."

"Do you have any extra fire starter?" Casha asked. "I think we will need the ability to keep warm more than we need food."

"I'm sure we can help you," Elb said. "But why not come with us, to Woodglen?"

"We really must keep going north." Gidley explained. "It's complicated, but we can't go back."

"Don't you have a tent?" Lorge asked. "I can't believe you are depending on trees for shelter, especially with this weather, at this time of year and heading northward. Why not go back and wait until spring?"

"We really do have to do this now," Gidley explained. "We are tracking some Elves, who have stolen something and the Queen has ordered us to find it and them.

"Oh, not good," Elb said. "Guess you're stuck with your quest."

"Where exactly are you headed?" Lorge asked.

"Well," Gidley began. "We don't know where we will end up, but the best lead we had when we started out was that they were headed north. It was good weather, when we left and we planned to stay at inns along the way. I guess we didn't plan this very well. I never thought of a tent. We've never done this before and like I said, we don't have a choice. We need to find the Queen's dagger, as soon as, possible. We may find the thieves we seek at the next town or village."

"Don't feel too bad. A tent might not have stood in this wind, anyway. Hey, Elb! Speaking of daggers, remember when we were at that inn this morning and those villagers were saying something about a dagger?" Lorge asked.

"Yeah, I remember something about that. Several of them were talking about an incident that had happened there and it involved a dagger," Elb replied. "Yeah, that guy that runs the stable said the Innkeeper got a good look at it. He said something about jewels. Go to the 'Good Elf Inn' here in Vallard when the weather breaks. It's probably three or four hours from here. It's in the Village of Good Elf, by the way. They may be able to help you."

"Oh, this is good news," Gidley said jumping up. "Thank you. This is the best news we've had. We at least know we're still on track, although we're about a week behind them."

"I'm sure the villagers remember those Elves, if they are the same ones you speak of. I'm sorry I didn't hear more of what was said, but we were anxious to put ourselves on our way and, of course, had no knowledge of you and your quest."

"Which reminds me. We should get going. We don't want to cross that river in this storm, at dark!" Elb said.

"We know what you mean," Bellina said. "I fell in because I didn't see the edge of the bridge. I caused our current problem."

Her friends assured her that it wasn't her fault. They really were ill prepared to start on the journey, in the first place. Gidley felt really bad about not thinking of a tent. He thought the whole trip was going badly, would probably get worse, and if they failed…well. He turned his thoughts to these two new acquaintances, who had given them some useful news, not to mention food and some fire starter.

When Elb handed Jinto a couple of carrots, Gidley only felt worse. He never thought once of that poor pony. He didn't remember carrots.

'I'm so awful at this,' he said to himself and looked at Casha. Apparently, he didn't say *that* out loud.

After the two Elves left, the group settled down to eat some of the food they had just been given.

A few hours later the wind died down and eventually stopped. They could see the sun peek out between thick clouds. It was setting and it was already getting dark and they didn't want to venture out now. They had hope that tomorrow would be clear. How they were going to get through the snow, no one knew.

Chapter 11

BEDS FOR THE NIGHT

It was indeed clear the next morning. The friends ate breakfast and gathered their belongings. They were leaving the cozy area that had been their home for the past three days and each was wondering how they were ever going to get through the snow and make it to Good Elf Village.

Gidley thought that the three or four hours they were told about, for the journey, would turn out to be a much longer time. After all, those guys were riding ponies.

"I guess we'd better get a move on, if we want to reach a warm bed tonight," Gidley called to them.

There were some mumbles all around, but no one made much of a comment.

The snow only amounted to about six inches, but because of the strong winds that had been blowing for the past three days the snow had drifted to one or two feet in some places, and the ground was laid bare, in others.

The next six hours were horrible for the little group. They had to stop frequently to rest and several times, had to seek shelter under a tree and build a small fire in order to warm themselves. The bitter cold made their traveling very hard.

They were cold, wet and hungry, when they reached the Good Elf Village, at dusk. They had been bone weary, but at the sight of the candles glowing in the windows, gave them a burst of energy strong enough to at least get them to the Inn.

Jinto led the poor, exhausted pony to the stable and everyone else went inside the Inn to get some food and warm beds for the night. They were all anxious to get a good bath.

At the Good Elf Inn

Elves make a marvelous soup of herbs and vegetables that is guaranteed to warm you on a cold night and, thankfully, the Innkeeper had a huge pot of it cooking over a grand fire, in the fireplace.

"My goodness, you look to be half dead," the Innkeeper exclaimed, with some concern. He was a jolly, fat Elf, with thinning, white hair and green eyes. "Sit down and let me get you some vita. You'll feel much better after you've had some. Soup's almost ready."

"Thank you, sir," Casha spoke first. "We need food, vita, a bath and a good nights sleep, in a warm bed. That storm caught us just past the Janego River and we've been held up under a fir tree, for three days."

"With no food?" gasped the Innkeeper.

"Oh, no, we had a little," Gidley said. "It's just been a rough trip."

"I'd say, I'd say. Here is your vita. I'll get the soup." And he hustled away.

It was a lovely old inn. Elves make and keep nice houses and their Inns are among the finest anywhere. Not that this group were adept travelers, but they had heard it many times from others passing through Sharrock.

The fireplace was massive. It held several pots suspended from hooks and wonderful smells came out and hit each visitor's nose. There were simple tables and stools placed around the room, and at one end of the room a dart-board was hung awaiting the nights players.

The bar was long and sleek and polished to a high shine. Scones were piled high on a platter at one end, covered with a thin cloth. Kegs of wine, ale and vita were stacked against the back wall. Tankards lined a shelf just below the bar. Everything here was clean and polished.

"That fireplace be the biggest I ever seen," said a wide-eyed Jinto, as he entered the Inn. "And me being a stonemason, like, well I built some big ones."

"Get the pony settled, okay?" asked Bellina.

"Oh, yes, ma'am. It's a right good stable they be having, like," Jinto answered. "I think he'll be happy to be there, like I'm happy to be here."

The Innkeeper returned with the soup and a lovely, warm, fragrant loaf of fresh baked bread.

"Ooh!" they all said at once.

While the party ate and warmed up, several others came into the inn. It was a very popular place. Apparently, the Innkeeper was well known for his delicious food and clean, attractive place.

After the meal was finished, the group sat quietly thinking and listening to the other guests. Everyone was talking and laughing and every so often, someone would sing or play their flute or fiddle. Several older Elves engaged, in what seemed like, a very serious game of darts.

When the Innkeeper came by to deliver more vita, Casha commented about how beautiful and clean everything was. The Innkeeper thanked her for the compliments and added that last week it was put into quite a state, what with the fight and murder of one of the village Elves.

"Oh, my," said Bellina. "What happened?"

"Some guys comin' from a big party down the south of us. Been drinkin' wine or ale and in a nasty state. They stop for food, but hardly eat anything. More interested in drinkin' and makin' rude comments to the ladies. Henly, the local weaver comes in and sits next to the big feller, at the bar. After a few minutes, Henly looks down and says, 'Mighty fancy dagger sheath, for the likes of you' and the guy tells him to shut up. Says he won the dagger from a guy at the party," the Innkeeper continued. "Anyway, Henly asks can he see the dagger and the guy lays it right there, on the top of the bar. Right there in front of Henly and me."

"Well, you never saw such a beautiful thing in your life. All silver and gold and jewels. Even on the sheath. Henly picks it up and the big guy grabs him and tells him to put it down. He says he never gave Henly no permission to touch it. Henly put it down and he says somethin' to the big guy and next thing, they were rollin' on the floor and then the big guy's friends get up to help and our guys get up to help Henly. Then there's a big fight. Lots of stuff broken."

"Suddenly, the fight stops as one guy grabs his knife and kills Henly, right there. They up and left and no body tried to stop them. No one wanted to die."

Gidley let out the breath he had been holding throughout the Innkeepers narrative.

"Do you know where they went? Or what their names were? Were there five of them?"

"Whoa, friend," the Innkeeper said, holding up his hands. "I'm just reportin' what I saw. Other than givin' them drinks, I didn't pay them no mind, at first, and afterward, well, afterwards we all tended Henly. Though it was too late to help him, I'm afraid. Stuck him dead he did."

"Is there anyone here tonight, who may have been in here that night?" Gidley asked.

"I'm sure most were," he answered.

"Anybody who may know, who those evil elves were?" Gidley persisted. "They are probably the ones we have been sent by Queen Findra to find, and we have no leads."

"Excuse me, everyone," yelled the Innkeeper. "Does anyone have any information, about those elves who stuck Henly to death?"

"You know we would a gone after them ourselves, if we did," someone yelled back.

"Does anyone know where they were going or where they were from?" Casha asked

"If we'd a knowed that, we'd a got 'em ourselves," someone else yelled. "Do you think we'd just sit around and not avenge Henly's death?"

"No, of course not," Casha tried again. "I apologize, it's just that we are desperate to find these five elves, who stole a priceless dagger."

The stableman had finished settling the ponies in his charge, for the night and had stopped at the inn for a bite to eat and a drink before going home. He heard Casha ask about the thieves, just as he came in the door.

"I don't know where they come from, other than a party south of here. Yes, there were five of 'em. One was called Bomid. I remember the name 'cause that's my brother. It weren't my brother, what stuck 'ole Henly, you understand," the stable man said. "It's just, I know the name. No mistake!"

"Bomid! Yes," said Gidley. "I remember that name. Wasn't one called Zirba?"

"I know one was called Odoman," said another Elf from the back of the room.

Everyone turned to look at him.

"Well, the big guy, the one stuck Henly, he said 'Odoman, let's get out of here'. I was standing right in back of him, when he said it."

"You all have helped us very much," Gidley said. "If we find them, we'll make sure they are punished. They are very evil."

A chorus of 'yeahs' answered Gidley. The friends talked to a few more villagers who told them the same story of Henly's murder, but not anything more helpful.

The friends did find out that Lord Rupert, the Ruler of Vallard, was asked to send out a group of soldiers, to look for the murderers. He refused, saying that he didn't want to spark a war with his neighbors, over a drunken brawl.

A few of Henly's friends were going to look for them, on their own, but Lord Rupert refused to let them go.

The travelers planned to go north toward Dawes, which was through the Baili Mountains. They were following the information that the stableman had given, that the five elves went north, when they rode out. Also, one of them was heard to say something about 'them in Dawes would be pleased to get the dagger'.

Dawes was ruled over by King Greybar. It was a Kingdom of Dwarves, who mine the Baili Mountains.

'Why would Elves be stealing daggers, for Dwarves?' Gidley wondered.

"Who knows," answered Dira, who was surprised by the look Gidley gave him.

The conclusion that they all came up with was, maybe, the thieves were going to try to sell the dagger or the gemstones to the Dwarves. Surely, as miners, the Dwarves would know the value of the gems.

"Maybe they just want to know what it's worth," Dira said.

"It's the only lead we've got and it makes sense that they would go to see the Dwarves, whatever their reason," Casha said.

The travelers went to sleep that night, in high spirits. Maybe their quest would be over quickly.

Chapter 12

THE SEARCH GOES ON

Gidley was the first one up the next morning and since everyone else seemed to need a little more sleep, he went down to have breakfast alone.

The Innkeeper wasn't there, but an Elf who turned out to be his wife, was, and she made a very good breakfast.

After breakfast, Gidley asked Mrs. Hymur to please make up some bundles of food to replace the ones they had lost. She sent him to see Dindle, whom she thought might be able to fix Gidley up with a new firebox and possibly a tent.

Dindle did indeed have a firebox, but only one small tent. It was only made to sleep two or three, but Gidley bought it anyway. You just never knew what might come in handy, in this travel-adventure thing.

'Everything will be okay', Gidley thought. 'Do not doubt yourself'.

Once everyone else was up and had started on their breakfast, Gidley filled them in on all that he had accomplished that morning.

They were proud of him and very grateful, that everything was taken care of so that they could load up the pony and go.

Although there was still some snow and it was windy, the sun continued to shine today and it was actually warmer than it had been for some time.

Everyone felt much better this morning. Yesterday's awful trip to get to the inn was made worse by cold, hungry Elves, who had spent three nights under a tree. Today's travelers were well rested and fed and all the supplies were back to the full side. And, they had a good idea where the murdering thieves and the dagger might be.

Bellina played them on their way.

The scenery didn't change much. There was just snow and trees and occasionally they saw the smoke rise from a chimney. There were more Elves in Vallard than there had been in Woodglen, though the houses seemed far apart. The travelers started to see the snow capped mountains rising in the distance.

After several hours and a few stops for food and rest, the group was finally getting close to the mountains.

There was an open field between them and the mountain, that looked to be about a mile wide, but they could see the opening that was the pass through, to the Dwarves' Kingdom of Dawes. In summer the field would be covered with wild flowers and graceful grasses, in winter, all that grew here was snow.

The mountains must have sheltered this area, for the snow wasn't very deep. Also, it appeared that someone or several someone's had gone this same route ahead of them and had beaten down what little snow there was.

They were all in good spirits until a sudden swooshing sound, like a strong wind, was heard.

Looking up, Bellina screamed.

Everyone froze and seeing her looking up, all turned their faces skyward. They all screamed. Well, Casha screamed. Everyone else gave a funny sounding grunt.

Diving straight at them were huge black birds or dragons. They couldn't really tell, because the sun was in their eyes. They couldn't see well, but they knew they were in danger. The field was flat, without even one tree or rock. There was no place to hide!

The pony whinnied and reared up, taking Jinto by surprise. Jinto fell and the pony tried to run. He stepped on Jinto and with the reins wrapped around Jinto's hand, the pony ran and pulled Jinto through the snow behind him.

Everyone else dropped to the ground, as the ugly birds swooped, screeching from the sky, with their talons extended.

Their wings were at least fourteen feet across and yet the birds were able to dive and fly easily.

As one flew over Casha, she looked into its face and saw piercing, golden eyes and a long, sharp beak just a few feet above her. She felt the air from the wings, brush over her body. She had never been so scared in her whole life.

Attack of the Drazils

One bird dove down towards Dira and was able to grab him and had lifted him, about six feet in the air, but Dira, struggling like a mad man, broke the grip and the bird dropped him. He lay still, with the wind knocked out of him, but what snow there was had broken his fall. He seemed okay.

Meanwhile, Jinto had gotten his hand free, but the pony had gone running, as fast as he could, heading back towards Vallard. Jinto followed after him, yelling for him to stop.

Gidley tried to stand up to help Dira, when one of the birds hit him on the arm and upper back with its claws. It didn't get a good grip, because Gidley had pulled his dagger, as he stood, and turning, stabbed, at the bird's feet and legs.

Bellina and Casha, seeing Gidley get attacked, pulled out their daggers and stood. Casha was knocked down before she ever got a chance to brace herself, and the dagger flew out of her hand.

Bellina stabbed at a bird and felt the dagger cut into something. It made a popping sound and the bird let out a screech and turned away.

By this time, Casha had found her dagger and she and Bellina stood back to back and defended themselves from further attack.

Gidley felt his arm start to sting and when he looked down, he saw that he was bleeding at a four-inch tear on his shirtsleeve. Pulling back the cloth, he saw a similar tear in his arm.

Just then, another bird grabbed him from behind, clutching him by the shoulders and lifted him off his feet. Gidley again stabbed with his dagger, and the bird dropped him. He came very close to falling on his own dagger. He lay still, out of breath, his heart beating so rapidly that he felt faint.

Reyal stabbed at every bird that swooped near him. He was recovering from the lupode bite and had made up his mind not to get bitten by these awful things.

Suddenly, the air was filled with a terrible screech. One bird made a funny turn and then fell from the sky. Another screech and another bird fell, spinning towards earth.

Everyone stood watching this amazing turn of events. What happened to the birds?

Chapter 13

DASH TO THE RESCUE

The remaining birds flew off. Still, no one could figure out what had happened until Reyal, who was closest to one of the fallen birds, went forward to investigate.

His mouth fell open and he turned to his friends.

"He's got an arrow stuck in him," Reyal exclaimed.

"An arrow?" asked Casha and Bellina.

"Yeah, it's definitely an arrow," Reyal answered.

"But…," Gidley stopped, as he saw the possible reason for the arrows, heading towards them, across the field.

"Uh, Casha, Bellina. Turn around," Gidley said, pointing in the direction of the Elf, who was now almost close enough to them to see his face.

"Hello," he called. "Is everyone all right?"

"Hello and thank you," Gidley yelled back.

They were all making their way toward where Gidley was standing and all arrived for introductions and for an assessment of their wounds.

"I am Dashel of Thorpshire," said the handsome Elf. "And I hope you aren't hurt badly. We should get you checked out and tend those wounds. I'm glad I arrived when I did."

"We are too," Bellina said.

She thought this Dashel was very nice, indeed! He was a little taller than Reyal, but he looked to be about the same age, as she, Casha and Gidley. He had light blond hair and big blue eyes and his cheeks were pink from the cold. He wore a rich, woolen cloak, dyed bright blue, which matched his eyes.

He handed Gidley a pouch of vita he had picked up, on his way over to them.

"Well, Dashel we surely owe you our lives," said Gidley extending his hand to the stranger. "Let's head towards the mountains, before our feathered friends come back. We can eat and tend our wounds there."

"You can call me Dash," the stranger said shaking Gidley's out stretched hand. "All my friends do. The only person, who calls me by my full name, is my mother! Let's do get out of here, before the drazils come back."

"I never heard of drazils, before," Gidley told him.

The others agreed that they hadn't either.

"That was pretty good shooting. You must be very good with that bow to hit them like you did," Reyal complimented him.

"Thanks," answered Dash. "I won't tell you how many arrows missed."

They all laughed and they walked, as fast as they could, and eventually made it safely to the shadows of the mountains.

Once there and somewhat calmer than before, the poor travelers made several startling discoveries.

The first was that Gidley was hurt pretty badly. The bird had indeed torn a gash on his arm, but it had also torn a few places on his back, as well. He took a sip from his vita pouch, which he had luckily been wearing on the opposite side of where the wounds were.

The second thing was that Dira had some puncture wounds, which were bleeding badly and he had fallen on his arm. They didn't know if it was broken, or just bruised. Dash made a sling for him, and Casha gave him some vita from her pouch. Dira had fallen on his pouch and split it open.

The third and most startling thing was that they finally realized, not only was Jinto not with them, but the pony with all the supplies was also missing.

Because Reyal had been previously injured, and Gidley and Dira were now hurt, Dash volunteered to start back across the field to look for Jinto and the pony.

He hadn't gone far, when he spotted an Elf heading in their direction.

He turned and yelled back to the group, "I think your friend is coming. I'll go meet him, in case he is also hurt."

"I'll come too," Bellina surprised, herself, by saying.

About fifteen minutes later, Bellina and Dash met a very upset Jinto.

"My pony be gone running off, like, ma'am," he said, close to tears.

His hand was red and swollen from being dragged by the reins. His face had a few scrapes too, but the worst thing was his obvious broken heart.

"I loved him, I did. I tried to follow him, but he runs better, him bein' a pony and all," Jinto said, his voice breaking. "Not only is he gone, but them supplies is with him. It's not his fault, like, 'cause them birds was big and scared him."

"Oh, Jinto," Bellina said, putting her arms gently around him. "I'm so sorry your pony ran off. I don't know what to say, except, we know it wasn't the pony's fault."

"I found somebody's bundle, on my way," Jinto added. "It's the only one I seen. How is everyone, like?"

"Let's head back to the others and I'll tell you, on the way," Bellina said. "Oh, by the way. This is Dash. He killed two birds with a bow and arrows. He saved us!"

"I be pleased to meet you, sir," Jinto said. "I'm glad you come along, like. Now miss Bellina, tell me how the others are."

They arrived back at the campsite and everyone sympathized with Jinto about the loss of the pony. Jinto said, and the others agreed, that if the pony ended up back in the town where they had just stayed, the people in town would recognize him and take care of him until they went back that way.

Their main concern, now, was that the extra food was gone again and the bundle with the crystals was also gone. So, they didn't have any money, and to Gidley, the worst thing was that the new tent was gone and he had never even gotten to try it!

Dash agreed to help them get through the mountains and into a town called Lumpor. Lumpor was a good-sized town built near the mines, in Dawes.

He said he had a friend there, named Mulop, who would help them. They could make whatever arrangements that, they and Mulop, agreed to for any repayment.

"I believe we should try to get some sleep," Dash said. "We'll have a rough day getting through those mountains with the cold wind, not much food, and nearly everyone wounded."

"We don't have any food, do we?" Gidley asked.

"I have a little food, " Dash said. "If we are careful, it should be okay. Lumpor isn't so far away that we would starve before we get there."

They found an area surrounded by boulders, that formed a wall right at the start of tomorrow's path.

Bellina discovered that the bundle Jinto had picked up was the one that held the blankets made from the Fairy material.

Everyone was happy with that discovery.

As the travelers wrapped themselves in their cloaks and blankets and lay by the fire, they all were warm and were able to sleep quite peacefully.

The next morning was clear and the sun shone brightly, but its warm rays didn't get all the way down to where the group sat, having a very small breakfast.

It was cold at Baili Mountain.

Dash asked Gidley, "I hope you don't mind, but may I know why you are all traveling northward, at this time of year?"

"Not at all," Gidley said. "You may even know of the ones we seek."

Each one told a part of the tale and of their adventures leading up to where they found themselves this morning.

"Why are your only weapons daggers?" Dash asked at the end of their tale. "Did you not think you might have need of a bow and some arrows?"

Gidley blushed, "I guess we are ill prepared. I've never traveled out of Sharrock. Neither have Casha and Bellina, nor the others, that I know of."

"We have knives for cutting up our food," said Casha. "We could use them as weapons, if we have to."

"I'm sorry, if I seem rude miss, but those knives are not weapons," Dash told her. "You should have swords or bows and arrows, as well as, your daggers. There are rough characters and wild creatures, and don't forget the drazils. Your daggers weren't really very effective against them."

"I don't know how to use a bow and arrow," Gidley admitted.

"No problem. I'll teach you, when we get to Lumpor. They make excellent bows and arrows there. That's where mine comes from. If you get further north to Kimbarton, you may want to look up a Gnome, by the name of Hebor, who lives in the town of Elbac. He makes some of the best swords you'll ever find. He can teach you how to fight with them, too. You all may need more help. The Elves you seek seem dangerous and don't seem to mind killing."

They all agreed that Dash was right. They hadn't planned well at all.

"Well, everyone. The mountains await us!"

Chapter 14

THE ROAD TO DAWES

The first several miles were uneventful and Dash, who was leading, stopped often so the wounded could rest. Bellina played a tune to help keep their spirits up. They took a break in the afternoon and ate a few bites of food. They knew if they didn't have any problems that they would be in Lumpor by tomorrow and could get more food, if Dash's friend could help them.

"Oh," said Casha. "I just realized that Jinto has the pouch of Special Vita from Queen Findra. It has her seal on the side. How lucky for us."

"Mr. Gidley give me his extra one," Jinto said. "Mine bein' smashed open when I was dragged. I never noticed it be the Special Vita. Lucky I didn't drink it."

"Dash picked it up," Gidley said. "Lucky for us, again."

Everyone agreed that Dash had more than saved them, and all vowed that they would be in his debt forever.

"What is so special about *this* vita?" Dash asked.

"The Queen gave it to us for our journey. It is vita, made by the Fairies of Kellenshire. It has powers to calm and help those who have serious wounds, to recover," Gidley explained. "It actually is called 'Lifewater', by the Fairies, although it won't help a mortal wound. We were saving it, in case we ever really needed it. It's a good thing you found it. It could save our lives someday."

Most human people believe, incorrectly, that Elves are immortal.

Elves just live for so long, that most human's lives pass long before an Elf's does. The 'Lifewater' was very necessary for survival. It was something the Kellenshire Fairies had learned to make with their magic. Unfortunately, they learned of it after the last war and it was made in such small quantities that it was reserved only for the most serious wounds.

"Were there other things given to you, with special powers, that got lost when the pony ran off?" Dash asked.

"No," Bellina answered him. "I was given this magic flute, which I keep with me all the time and Casha has the power to reason and say the right things. Of course, Gidley had the dagger. We told you about them. They are our gifts from the Queen."

"What does the magic flute do?" Dash wanted to know.

"Just plays beautiful, soothing music," Bellina said.

"Ah, well, I've heard it and it was beautiful," he said, smiling at her. "My friends, the day passes, we should get going."

They all packed up their few belongings and started off again.

Gidley pondered the questions Dash had asked and he felt even less a leader than before. He realized he didn't fully understand how they were supposed, to do the things the Queen expected of them.

He knew he would definitely have to learn to shoot a bow and arrows and maybe even sword fight. The others would have to learn too. He, Dira and Reyal were hurt.

'How are we going to learn anything now?' he wondered.

"It will be fine," Casha said.

Gidley just shook his head.

Reyal pulled out his flute and played softly as they walked along.

The footing got harder, as they climbed higher. The path was rough and rocks were buried under the snow and ice. Suddenly, Casha slipped and slid about fifteen feet, before being stopped by a large rock jutting out, into the path.

She lay still and everyone feared she was badly hurt. Dash was the first to reach her, and he gently lifted her hand and called her name. Her eyes fluttered open and Dash asked her where she hurt. He gently slipped his hand, behind her head and started to help her lift it up.

At that moment, Gidley felt unreasonable anger, at Dash.

'Why is he helping her?' Gidley asked himself. "I think I should be the one to tend to her," he said aloud. "I'm responsible for everyone here, not you!"

"Oh, I'm sorry," Dash said, as he carefully removed his hand, from behind Casha's head. "I just meant to help."

"I'm sure you've done enough," Gidley said, as he knelt beside Casha.

He brushed the hair from her eyes, and after she assured him, that she was just shaken up a little, he helped her stand.

"Why, Gidley," Casha whispered to him. "I've never heard you speak to anyone, like you did to Dash. "What ever was wrong?"

"He, he was helping you," Gidley said.

"So what, he certainly helped us before," she insisted.

"He helped everyone before. This time it was just you. I, I guess I got, you know, jealous," he explained, suddenly embarrassed.

"Jealous, Gidley?" Casha asked, smiling at him.

"Hey you two! If Casha's okay, can we go now?" Bellina called to them.

"Yeah, I'm good. I'm a little wet and dirty and I tore my pants a little, but we can go. Come on Gidley," Casha said and giggled, as she gave a little skip, away from him.

She turned her head back towards him and gave him a quick wink.

Dash smiled, as the reason for Gidley's sudden hostility explained itself.

The travelers continued through the mountain pass, and even occasionally going through some deep snow, they made better time than they thought they would. There were no more problems and they arrived at the base of the mountain, about five miles from the town of Lumpor.

After a quick stop to rest and have a sip of vita, they continued on to the town.

Lumpor was pleasant looking, with close-set houses, on a wide road that ran straight through town. On the other side of the town the houses, all small cottages, began to thin out. This was a country of miners and there didn't appear to be any large farms, like in Sharrock. Each family grew what they needed, in gardens next to their homes.

Chapter 15

A WELCOME IN LUMPOR

Dash led the party up to neat cottage, nestled in a grove of trees. There was a fenced area, on one side that Dash pointed out to them, saying that, in warm weather, lush flowers and a huge assortment of fruits, berries and vegetables grew there, tended by a master gardener.

Dira, being a farmer, said he wished he could see it in the late spring or summer and called out the names of several trees and shrubs that he recognized growing there.

At Dash's knock, an old Dwarf opened the door. He stood about three feet tall and had a big, round nose and close set, twinkling eyes and a long, white beard that reached, almost to his belt. He wore brown pants and a long green tunic that came within inches of his knees. Wrinkles disappeared when he broke into a huge smile at the sight of Dash standing there.

"Dash! What brings you here? I didn't expect to see you until next week."

"I've led some new friends here," Dash explained. "They are in need of help."

"Welcome to my home. Come in from the cold," Mulop said, as he opened the door wide and beckoned them inside."

It was a cozy one-room cottage, with a large fireplace and hearth in the middle of the back wall. It smelled of wood smoke, pipe tobacco and herbs. Mulop's bed was on one side, piled high with feather bedding. A table and some chairs stood on the other side where the kitchen was. Chairs and stools and small tables were grouped around the fireplace.

Mulop welcomes the travelers

Everyone entered and Mulop took their cloaks and directed them to the fireplace. He had been sitting there, himself, having a drink and a smoke before they arrived. The pipe still smoldered in a dish, on a small table.

"What would you like to drink and are you in need of food? Yes, of course, you are. Just sit, I'll get something for you. Oh, how many? Six and Dash. One moment."

Mulop asked and answered his own questions faster than anyone else could answer for him.

"May we help?" Casha asked and indicated that Bellina would help also.

"Would I want my guests to help? No, of course not. Sit, please. Dash, keep your friends over by the fire," Mulop called out.

Mulop began setting out bread and honey and pots of preserved fruit. He had a large tankard of ale and small, sweet cakes.

"Now, come get some food. You can bring what you like over near the fire. I must hear your tale. What brings you here?" he asked.

They all waited for him to answer himself and laughed, when they realized he actually was asking them a question.

Mulop looked confused a minute, but Dash explained what they found so funny.

"Oh, my. I am always doing that. Come, come, eat. I'm impatient to find out what my dear friend has brought me."

After introductions all around, each traveler took a turn explaining a part of the story. They told of why they were there, and just how they did manage to make it thus far. When they reached the part about Dash killing the drazils, Mulop's eyes lit up. He was proud of Dash's skill with the bow and arrow.

"Oh, my lad, a drazil is hard to kill. They are very large, no doubt, but they are also swift and deadly. Those nasty little Moards keep them around. I think they have trained them and they ride them when they have a long way to travel. Were there Moards attacking you, too? You didn't mention them, so probably not. Go on," Mulop implored them.

"Wait a minute," Bellina interrupted. What the heck is a Moard? I've never heard of them."

"Moards are Goblin-like creatures, nasty, as I say. They live up there, in the mountains. They mine our old, abandoned shafts," Mulop told her. " They have named their city, country, whatever they call it, Yanog. There's more and more drazils we see, in the distance, all the time. They don't come around here much. We would shoot them out of the sky. Go on. What next?"

"Well, as we said, most of the food was lost when the pony ran off. Some of them have wounds, which need tending, and they need bows and arrows. Oh, and you and I need to teach them how to shoot them. And, oh yes, they have no way of paying. They need crystals," Dash explained, in one breath.

"Is there anything else?" Mulop asked, laughing and throwing his hands up.

Gidley swallowed his sweet cake and said, "One more thing. Have you seen five Elves ride through here in the last couple of weeks?"

"Five Elves? Yes, of course. Nasty creatures. We think they stole some food and crystals, but no one was really sure. We don't have much trouble around here. No one really keeps anything locked up. You know, I didn't talk to them, but I may have seen them in town. Let me go get my friend Dorcat. Those guys were at the tavern and asked him some questions. Didn't mean anything to either of us, at the time, but now…just wait."

Mulop left the cottage to get his friend.

"This could be our big break," Dira said.

"I hope so, " Gidley added. "So far, we haven't learned much. I'm afraid we may never find the dagger."

"We'll find those thieves and the dagger, Gidley," Casha said, smiling at him. "We just need some time and a little luck."

"Gidley, what be happening to us, like, if we don't get the dagger?" Jinto asked.

"Yeah, can we go home, again?" Dira wanted to know. "Me and Reyal have families and we were just wondering."

"I imagine everyone can go home, except me," Gidley said, sadly.

"And, me," added Casha. She gave Gidley a smile.

Just at that moment, the door opened, bringing Mulop, his friend Dorcat and a blast of cold air.

Dorcat was, about the same height as Mulop, but his hair and beard were a silver- gray and when he pulled his cap off, his hair jumped up, into wild looking wisps. He had a pleasant look about him and bright, almost dancing eyes. He was dressed just as Mulop was, in brown pants and tunic, except his tunic was bright red.

"Here are the Elves I told you about. Sit and tell them what you know about the five evil Elves with the dagger," Mulop urged his friend.

He introduced them and Dorcat sat and began his tale.

"One night, maybe two weeks ago, I'm sittin' in the tavern, see. I'm havin' some ale, which I could use right now, Mulop. When in comes these Elves. Oh, thanks. Umm, best ale, in Lumpor. So, in comes these Elves and you could see they was mean. They didn't talk nice when they ordered their drinks. Mind if I have a sweet cake? Ooh, very good. So, these Elves drink a while and one of 'um, Zirba, I think he said, comes over and starts asking me about the mines around here, if I'm a miner, I say 'yes' and do I get good gems. 'Yes' I say again, then he starts asking me about, now this is funny, I don't mean, to laugh at funny, just plain *odd* funny. He says 'Do you know what a kimbar is?' and I have to think a minute. Then I says, 'I remember hearing about them, but I never saw one'."

"I remember one of the Elves telling me about kimbars, the night the dagger was stolen," Gidley said.

"They are very rare. No more kimbars have been mined, in my life time," Mulop added.

"Yeah, well that's what I thought was odd," continued Dorcat. "What would these Elves be doin' askin' about a rare stone, that only would show up in very expensive pieces, made years ago. I thought they was up to no good, so I tells them 'maybe you should go up to Kimbarton and ask the Gnomes, there'. The only place kimbars ever come from was the Magenta Mountains, in Kimbarton. That's how they get their name, not the gems, the Realm. Never had none here, in the Baili Mountains, did we Mulop?"

"Not that I ever heard of. I hear our King Greybar has a couple in his crown. They were given to the Kingdom of Dawes many years ago, by King Ryin of Kimbarton, as a token of peace between our kingdoms. Those Gnomes are great with metal. They sent some of them down here to add the stones into the crown, themselves, or so I hear," Mulop told them.

"Did the Elves in the tavern show you the dagger?" Bellina asked.

"No, miss. I never did see the fancy dagger you folks are seeking," Dorcat told her. "I wish I *could* see it. It must be a wonderful thing."

"Do you know any of the history or who made the dagger, Gidley?" Dash asked him.

"I only know the little bit of history, that those guys told me that night, before they stole it. I don't know if any of it was true. They just said the stones were rare and it was made by a wizard," Gidley answered.

"A wizard? Who?" a startled, Mulop asked.

"I don't remember his name, if they even told me. But, they said it had a spell cast on it."

"Well, I know why Queen Findra is anxious for you to find it and bring it back to Sharrock. I just wonder why she gave it to you, in the first place. No offense, sir, but that dagger must be priceless," Mulop said.

"I know," said Gidley. "I'm trying to get it back. It's called *The Dagger of Bahyel* and it goes to a hero. I just happened to have saved the life of the last hero to own it. I didn't ask for this."

"*The Dagger of Bahyel* was indeed, made by a wizard, and I have heard of the spell," Dorcat said, opening his eyes wide, in amazement.

"There's all kinds of stories and myths about *that* dagger," Mulop added, throwing his hands in the air. "You never said it was *The Dagger of Bahyel* you were hunting! You must get to sleep. We must be up early to start your training. It's more important than ever, now!"

Chapter 16

TRAINING AND TRAVELING

When Gidley awoke the next morning, he heard voices outside behind the cottage. Mulop had left a roaring fire in the fireplace and breakfast was laid out on the table. There was fresh bread and honey and pots of clotted cream and more of Mulop's wonderful preserves.

Gidley piled a little of everything on a thick slice of bread and went to see what Dash and Mulop were doing outside.

When he joined them, Gidley found that they had set up a board near the edge of the woods and Dash and Mulop were shooting arrows at a small circle they had marked in the center of it.

They were both very good. Gidley was still a little mad at Dash for tending Casha up on the mountain pass, but he knew it wasn't Dash's fault if he found Casha desirable. And reluctantly, Gidley realized that Dash had really helped them and that he needed Dash's skills, with a bow and arrow, in order to protect his friends from any more perils that they might still encounter.

Just then Dash turned around and saw Gidley standing there.

"Gidley, come on over," Dash called. "See if your arm is well enough to try this."

"It's better today," Gidley told him. "That stuff Mulop made out of herbs and rubbed on me really took the pain away."

"I'll give you some more before you go, " Mulop said. "I'm afraid with all your miss-adventures so far, you may have need of it. Don't you think? Yes, I'm sure you do."

"Yes, I'm afraid so," Gidley said. "I'm not a good leader and I feel ill prepared."

Bellina and Jinto shooting arrows

"Well, we are ready to prepare you," Dash said, laughing.

"Do you use your right or left hand?" asked Mulop.

"Right," Gidley told him.

"Oh, good, Mulop said. "Most of the strain is on your right hand and your wounds are on the left!"

Between Dash and Mulop, Gidley got the best one-hour training anyone could have given him.

As Gidley trained, one by one, the other friends came outside and more boards were set up and soon, all were firing arrows towards them. Not all of the arrows were hitting the boards, in fact, a lot of them never even made it down that far.

Jinto, it turned out was the best shot, so far. He had the steady hands and strength, and just plain, old, good aim.

Dira couldn't even try because his arm, while not as sore, was still swollen and in the sling. He watched his friends a while, but feeling useless he went back inside and sat by the fire and awaited their return.

Reyal had a hard time and Dash feared he would end up losing his nose. Reyal held the bow at an odd angle, next to his nose, and Dash winced every time Reyal pulled back on the string. They would show him the correct position, but then he would move his arm. Dash couldn't wait for lunchtime so they could quit.

Casha did a pretty good job, but it was Bellina who really took to the bow and arrow like she had waited all her life for it.

By the end of the afternoon, Dash and Mulop agreed that Jinto and Bellina were the foremost archers.

The fact that Casha and Gidley were 'pretty good' wasn't good enough for Mulop, but Dash pointed out that the group needed all the help they could get. They knew the basics and would be able to help to defend themselves. He knew they would get better with practice.

As everyone settled down to a well-deserved supper, Mulop was generous with his praise for their days work.

Dash was so proud of Bellina. He never knew any female Elves, where he came from, who could shoot like that.

They all spent the next whole day practicing and even Mulop said he felt that they were ready to go on with their travels. They had a good defense team now.

The following morning the friends prepared to leave.

Mulop gave them food and a tankard, of his ale. Gidley, Casha and Bellina didn't like the ale, as it made them dizzy, but Jinto, Dira and Reyal found it quite good and a nice change, from always having vita.

They were also given a small sack of crystals and a few other small gemstones in case they had to buy food or stay at an Inn. He also told them to keep the bows, that each had used the past two days and gave them a large supply of arrows.

Mulop said that ponies were hard to come by and the ones they had were needed in the mines, so, as sorry as he was, there were none to spare.

Gidley told him not to worry, they were used to carrying their own bundles and he didn't want anything happening to another pony, anyway.

Everyone else agreed with him.

Mulop and Gidley shook hands on an agreement that Mulop would come visit them, when they got back to Sharrock and if they would feed him and put him up, it would be payment enough.

They were all more than happy with that arrangement.

After looking at the map, they knew they were heading to the town of Elbac in Kimbarton and that they had a long, long journey ahead.

The bad news was that Dash announced that he had some business for his father in Lumpor, which was why he was headed this way originally and that once that was done, he had to go home. He said that, as much as he would like to, he couldn't go with them on their quest. He reminded them to look up the Gnome, named Hebor, for the swords and asked them to please let him know how they made out.

"I would love to see this amazing dagger," he told Gidley. "I had never heard of it before. I can't wait to tell my Father about it and ask if he's heard of it."

They all thanked Mulop, again, for everything he had done for them and asked him to thank Dorcat for his help.

"Well, I may be seeing you back through here, in a week or so, unless your travels take you in another direction. I'd appreciate you letting Dorcat and I have a look at that dagger, once you get it back," Mulop said. He grabbed Gidley and gave him a hug, mindful of the wounds.

"Be safe, my little friend, and keep the rest of the bunch together safe and sound. They are good, loyal friends. You can do it, because you are becoming a fine leader."

' Oh, yeah,' thought Gidley, 'I'm a fine leader, if I don't get us all killed.' He looked quickly to see, if there was a reaction from anyone. No one said anything and Gidley smiled to himself. 'At least I'm getting better at something.'

Gidley felt he should apologize to Dash for his behavior on the mountain pass. That outburst was uncalled for. He started his apology, but Dash stopped him.

"I understand about Casha," Dash said. "I meant only to help her up. Don't worry about it. No apology is necessary. I've already forgotten it."

Gidley smiled and nodded. He was surprised when Dash gave him a quick hug and wished him well.

Dash bade them all farewell and good luck and, as he turned to go back towards Mulop's house, the rest of the group turned north.

The day was warm again and a lot of the snow had melted. Walking was a little easier and there was a good, clear road all the way to Elbac. At least they wouldn't get lost.

Bellina pulled out her flute and played them out of town.

Even with everyone feeling much better and taking few breaks, they still had not made it to Kimbarton, by nightfall.

"Well," said Gidley, "I guess we find a tree to sleep under. We lost our tent and we didn't buy another one in that town, Vokore, we passed two hours ago.

"Oh, Gidley," Dira laughed. "You are going to worry yourself into your grave over getting a tent."

Everybody laughed, even Gidley.

They were able to find a nice sheltered area near some thick shrubs. They built a fire and wrapped themselves in their cloaks and blankets.

All night they kept hearing the wailing sounds of lupodes, but none came near the fire. They took turns on watch, this night. They were near the Great North Forest and they feared the lupodes, who lived there. It seemed the further they got from home the more the dangers increased.

Chapter 17

SWORDPLAY

The following morning, as the travelers awoke and had breakfast, they spoke about hearing the lupodes all night.

"I killed one," Bellina said. "And the rest finally took off."

"You killed one? How? Did it come near the campsite?" they all asked.

"No, it didn't come real close, but it came within range of my trusty bow and arrow," Bellina explained.

"How could you see?" Gidley asked, incredulously.

"I just aimed for those beady red eyes, that I could see glaring at me. There was enough moonlight, for them to really shine."

"How do you know you killed him?" asked Casha.

"This morning, when it got light I went and looked. He's dead," Bellina said, proudly.

They all congratulated her, but the one person she wished could be there, wasn't. He would soon be going home and according to the map 'his home' wasn't anywhere near where they were going.

Once they were packed up and ready to go, they all walked over to see Bellina's lupode. She had, indeed, killed him.

As they began this day's journey, Jinto started singing a song that they all knew from home. At first, it made them all a little homesick, but as he continued with his rich melodious voice, Reyal and Bellina joined in with their flutes, and then Casha's sweet voice joined in and their music filled the air.

Casha and Jinto sounded really good together. Gidley and Dira kept quiet and just enjoyed it.

With the Baili Mountains behind them, the travelers could now see the tops of the Magenta Mountains, looming up ahead. As they walked along they were all in good spirits.

Kimbarton was almost the exact opposite of Dawes. Dawes started with the miners and as they went further north, gradually the Dwarves of the other towns, became the builders and farmers and providers, of other goods. Here the miners were very far, to the north, where the mountains were.

That afternoon they arrived in Elbac.

Elbac had a large cluster of homes and shops, on one end of the town as you entered. Going through the town, few houses lined the road going north, toward the mountains and the town of Lemet, which was where King Ryin's Palace was located.

There wasn't an inn, but a nice lady Gnome showed them where her sister lived and told them that her sister took in travelers, when there were any.

"Not many comes this way," she told them. "Too far north, for most folks."

They found the neat white house, with the wide front porch and what looked to be a garden, on the side. At least, in spring, it would be.

The knock on the door brought a lovely older Gnome lady, with snow-white hair and deep blue eyes. She was dressed in a long woolen skirt and wool shirt and she wiped her hands, on an apron tied at her waist.

"And what may I do for you?" she inquired, as she smiled a great, comforting smile.

They explained that her sister had pointed her home out to them, as a place to stay the night. She opened the door wide and let them inside.

It was a simple, but clean home, with a roaring fire in the fireplace and comfortable looking chairs all around. It smelled like apples and lemons.

Gidley discussed payment, using Mulop's gems and the lady, Mrs. Baloc, went to get beds and a bath ready for them and to prepare their supper. They all collapsed in the chairs, until supper was ready.

The food was delicious and everyone was grateful that there would be beds and nice soft feather filled coverlets. The nights at Mulop's house were spent on the floor, (even though he tried to give his bed to Casha and Bellina, while he joined the others, on the floor) and last night outside was cold, uncomfortable and just plain scary. Beds would be nice indeed.

After supper Mrs. Baloc settled them in front of the fireplace and brought them tea and sweet cakes.

"We are looking for five Elves. Very, very bad Elves who might have come through, about two or three weeks ago," Gidley told her.

"I don't recall seeing any Elves, other than yourselves," Mrs. Baloc said. "We notice things like that, around here. Besides, I have the only sleeping house here and I got no Elves. We live on the only road from here to the next town, which is quite a long way and leads only to the palace. East there's nothing but forest."

"Can you tell us where we might find a man named Hebor?" Dira asked her. "We were told to look him up by friends in Lumpor."

"Oh my," laughed Mrs. Baloc. "That's my sister's husband and as you know, they live just down the road from here! I believe you already passed the house you seek."

"We hear he is an excellent swordsman," Casha added.

"Not just *any* swordsman, although there be none better, but he makes the finest swords, daggers and knives around," Mrs. Baloc added, proudly.

"I think I'll run down there and see if he can talk to me tonight," Gidley said. "I'm anxious to talk to him about the possibility that he may have been contacted by the evil Elves we seek and to see if he can arrange to teach us some sword fighting, or at least give us a quick lesson like Dash and Mulop did.

"I'd like to go along, if you don't mind," Reyal said. "I've always been interested in swords. My father used to tell me stories about the war and the swordsmen were my favorite fighters."

"Of course, please come," Gidley said, "And before anyone else asks, No! I want you to stay here and rest. We won't be long."

"I'm giving them a dose of my special tonic," Mrs. Baloc told him. "They are going to tell me their adventures and then they are off to sleep. Don't stay out too long. You both get tonic and bed, when you return."

Gidley felt like saying 'yes, mommy', but he knew that wouldn't be very nice. Instead, he told her he appreciated her care and concern for him and his friends.

Gidley and Reyal found Hebor at his home, and they were welcomed in.

His wife was glad to see them again and inquired about their stay at her sister's home. She also had a clean comfortable home and it smelled like apples and lemons too!

'Must be a family thing,' thought Gidley.

"What family thing?" Hebor asked.

Blushing, Gidley said, "Ah, the way the houses smell like, ah, apples and lemons"

Both Hebor and his wife laughed and nodded, but neither explained the smell.

Hebor's wife looked so much like her sister that they could be twins. Hebor, who stood about three feet tall, looked a lot like Mulop, except Hebor had a short, neatly trimmed beard and a long mustache that curled up at the ends. Mulop had small round ears, but Hebor had the largest ears Gidley had ever seen. His nose, although round and reddish like Mulop's, was smaller and he had cheekbones that puffed his face out like he had grapes stuck in there.

While his wife got some tea, Hebor asked them what it might be that they needed from him.

Gidley and Reyal briefly explained their mission and asked Hebor, if he could help them. Gidley asked about the possibility of the thieves having been through there.

"I haven't seen any Elves, other than yourselves, come through here in more than a month. The last ones were a young couple looking to buy a knife, as a gift for the woman's brother, who had just joined King Handor's army. They left right after the purchase and turned towards their home."

After some discussion, Hebor told Gidley that if Dash had not heard of these evil Elves, they probably didn't come from Thorpeshire. He said that they most likely came from Dordom, west of them.

"The whole place is evil. I'd put my money on them being from there," Hebor said. "No good ever came from that realm."

Gidley sighed. They were going the wrong way.

Hebor told them that he had, indeed, heard of *The Dagger of Bahyel*, but he had never seen it.

"You couldn't be the master maker of weapons without hearing of all the ancient, priceless works of art," Hebor told them. "That one, I believe, has been talked about many times, but it has stayed in the Kingdom of Sharrock and has been seen by very few. There are even rumors that it doesn't exist."

"Oh, it exists all right," Gidley assured him. "I just have to find it, while it still does."

After they answered all the questions Hebor asked of them, he took them out to a separate building, behind his house. Gidley and Reyal were astounded at the array of swords, knives and daggers hanging on the walls and laid out on a large table, covered with green velvet. Reyal was just standing there, with his mouth open.

He managed to say, "My dream come true!"

Hebor laughed and slapped him, on the back, saying, "Pick one up and try it."

"Oh, no, I couldn't," Reyal said in a whisper. "I'll wait until we have our lessons."

While Hebor had some very beautiful daggers, none could compare with the dagger they sought. Gidley didn't mention that, however.

Gidley made arrangements for lessons and because the swords were expensive, Hebor suggested they only purchase swords for those who would actually turn out to be good enough to warrant spending the money.

"No sense someone dragging around a useless sword," Hebor explained. "Some people don't have the agility to move the way you must, to be a successful swordsman."

They shook hands and agreed to meet at Hebor's house early in the morning.

The others were already in bed by the time Gidley and Reyal returned. Mrs. Baloc gave them a big dose of tonic and sent them off to bed, too.

Gidley lay awake a long time thinking of all that had happened to them and about how little they had actually accomplished in their search for the dagger.

The following morning found everyone, except Gidley, up and in good spirits and ready for their lessons. Reyal was so excited he could hardly eat, so he spent the time instead telling his friends what had gone on at Hebor's house the night before.

Just as Dira decided he had better go wake Gidley, he appeared in the doorway, dressed and ready to go.

Casha grabbed two scones and piled clotted cream and preserves on them and handed them to Gidley on their way out the door.

Gidley thanked her and ate them just to please her, but he wasn't hungry and they felt heavy in his stomach. He still had to tell his friends that they were going the wrong way and he wasn't sure sword fighting was for him. He knew he needed to learn the skill, however, because according to Hebor, they were going to need all the help they could get. Dordom was a place of evil.

Hebor was ready for them when they arrived at his home. He had prepared the swords with leather sheaths so that they wouldn't cut themselves or each other, as they practiced the moves.

He did caution them that a blow to the head or body would definitely hurt or kill them, if delivered too enthusiastically. He set about explaining the sword's balance and showing them the moves, in slow motion.

Then he gave each of them swords and moved them far enough apart, to be able to swing the swords, without knocking out their neighbor.

Dira found that his arm and hand was too weak, still, to hold the sword properly and Gidley also found that his shoulder was still pretty sore.

Hebor advised Dira to drop out of the training and to just use his dagger, until his arm healed. He was afraid Dira might do permanent damage trying to swing the heavy sword. The others could show him all that they learned, if he became able to use his arm.

Dira felt more useless, now, than he did when Mulop and Dash dismissed him. He went back to Mrs. Baloc's house and she fed him and they sat and talked for the rest of the afternoon.

Hebor worked with Gidley on the moves, because he sensed how swift and agile Gidley was. Remembering that he had a mock wooden sword, which was lighter than the real thing, Hebor fetched it from his shop. Gidley had a much easier time of it after that.

Bellina seemed able to handle the sword well enough, but it was Reyal who was the star pupil, with Casha showing signs of being very good.

By afternoon, Casha and Reyal were mock fighting and everyone else was still practicing swinging the sword with both hands and trying to keep control.

Casha and Reyal practice sword fighting

Bellina and Jinto got the basics down, in case they ever needed to use a sword, but with Hebor's permission they went to a near by field and shot arrows for the rest of the afternoon.

It was getting dark before Hebor let them all go back to Mrs. Baloc's house for some much needed rest and food. Hebor was much more intense in his teaching, than Dash and Mulop had been.

Before they left, Hebor and Gidley came to an agreement over payment for the three swords that were needed for Casha, Reyal and Gidley and for the lessons.

Gidley was grateful for Mulop's crystals.

Back at Mrs. Baloc's, they ate ravenously and all headed off to bed early. Hebor wanted Casha, Gidley and Reyal, at his house as early as possible, the next morning.

When morning arrived, the beautiful sun filled days of the past week had been replaced with gray, thick clouds and a sharp cold in the air.

By noon it was snowing, and all the travelers felt a let down in their hearts. This meant hard traveling and being cold again.

Gidley had told them last night about the discussion with Hebor and the fact that they were going wrong and would have to head southwest, to get to Dordom. The friends took the news better than Gidley thought they would.

Now that it was snowing harder, they all agreed that they had better get started back towards the large Fairy settlement known as Delightment. It was ruled over by Queen Zerena, whom Mrs. Baloc was sure was the sister of Queen Sennabelle. She said it was good news for them and they would be welcomed, as travelers from near her sister's realm. She told them that since Dordom was a long way from where they were now, she suggested that they seek food and shelter from Queen Zerena, in Fala.

They hoped to cover as much ground as possible, before the snow got too deep or darkness overtook them. After a quick bite to eat, and with their new swords hung in sheaths over their backs, they bade Mrs. Baloc farewell.

She hugged them all and told them to come visit again. No charge.

"You get that dagger back and bring it here for me to see," she told them.

They promised to do their best and thanked her for everything.

She handed them all bundles of food and they turned south, for the first time since they began their adventure. As the group passed Hebor's house, he came out to see them off and wish them good luck.

"Gidley, this is for you," Hebor said, handing him a large bundle. "I have no use for it, as my traveling days are long past."

"Thank you," said Gidley, "but no gift is necessary."

"Yes it is," Hebor said with a big grin. "It's my tent. I've heard you really want one."

Everyone laughed except Gidley. He didn't think a tent was all that funny.

Checking out the map, they realized that they had to go southwest a while and then north to try to reach the town of Fala, which is where Queen Zerena had her marvelous crystal palace. It was the envy of all the Kings and Queens in the surrounding countries.

While the Fairy Queen's palace was too small for any of them to actually live in, they all would have liked to have the beautiful palace duplicated, in large scale, for themselves. It was so lovely that it made their castles, while grand, look ugly by comparison. None had the wealth or magic to build a palace entirely out of crystals, however.

After Mrs. Baloc had told them about the palace, they all were eager to see it and discussion about it occupied most of their conversation during the journey that day.

Chapter 18
WHAT HAPPENED TO BELLINA?

The group made their way slowly, as the snow continued to fall and it got darker. They had been walking for hours and everyone was getting cold, wet and tired.

Gidley thought it was time they found a suitable place to set up the tent and get some food and build a warm fire.

"Keep a look-out, for a campsite," Gidley called back, to the group.

"Pardon, me, but it be getting' a bit dark to go lookin' for a place suitable, like," Jinto yelled back to him.

"Jinto's right," Bellina added. "Let's just stop. I'm cold and I could just drop dead right here."

Casha, Gidley and Reyal had fought with their swords all morning and had already tired themselves out, long before they started on this part of the trip. Casha kept quiet, because she knew everyone was tired and she didn't want anyone mad at her.

"There's a small wood, off to the left," Dira shouted.

"Okay, everyone, let's get over there to that stand of trees that Dira pointed out," Gidley announced.

"Thank you!" Bellina said.

They all trudged over and using their feet, pushed and moved, as much snow as they could, in order to set up the tent Hebor had given them.

Reyal and Jinto set the tent up, while Gidley supervised and beamed.

He felt he was doing all he could for the group, by trying to get them to their destination safely and now, he was preparing shelter for them.

It apparently didn't dawn on Gidley that not only was he the reason for the trip, but he also was gaining the knowledge of travel, protection and shelter from all the various people he had met so far, on his journey.

Dira and Casha were inside the tent stamping down the snow, while Reyal, Jinto and Gidley gathered some leaves and evergreen boughs to put on the tent floor, so they could sleep, without lying directly on the cold, wet ground.

Bellina set about gathering some dry wood, from under the evergreen trees in order to get a fire started. She left her pouch of vita, her food bundle and her bow and arrows, in the tent, taking only her dagger and of course, her flute.

As she wandered further into the trees looking for drier areas, she didn't realize that she was out of sight of the others. Emerging, from under an evergreen tree with an armload of broken branches, she noticed how dark it had suddenly gotten and she couldn't see which way the tent was.

She fought down a moment of panic and realized that she needed to head out of the trees and once she was in the open, again, she would see the tent or maybe they had gotten a fire started and she would see the glow.

She had her flute, so she could always sound some notes. Surely they would hear that.

'Didn't music carry in the air?' she asked herself.

Once out from under the trees, Bellina looked around. It was so dark now, that looking back towards the trees, she couldn't be sure she had even come out of the small forest on the correct side.

'Don't panic,' she thought.

She drew her dagger, more as a comfort, than for protection. There wasn't anything around.

"I'll walk back to the trees and then circle around, until I find everyone," she said, to the night.

Now that she had a sensible plan, she began walking back towards the trees. The wind had picked up and came swooshing around her. She wrapped her cloak tighter around her body and went forward.

The blow, when it came, hit her so hard that she was knocked face down, in the snow. Her dagger flew from her hand. A moment later she was plucked from the ground and carried so high, so quickly, that she never had the chance to scream. By the time she caught her breath and did scream, she was too high and too far away for her friends to hear her.

A drazil had her firmly grasped in it's claws and he was carrying her towards the top of the mountains.

Bellina began to cry. She was more afraid than she had ever been in her life. How could her friends find her? They wouldn't miss her for a while and when they did, it would be too late at night to look for her and they wouldn't have a clue that a drazil had carried her up to the mountains. They weren't even headed this way.

'Do drazils eat Elves?' she wondered, and her mind said 'yes', why else would it have grabbed her. Then she remembered the Moards.

Meanwhile, back at the campsite, Gidley began to get a little nervous when he realized Bellina hadn't come back to the tent with the firewood. He quickly asked Casha, to begin building a fire with the leaves they had brought back for their beds. He pulled Reyal aside and pointed out that Bellina hadn't returned yet.

"I noticed," Reyal said. "We had better start calling for her."

"I didn't want to panic everyone," Gidley explained. "I thought we, you and I, could go look for her."

"It's dark and cold and snowing," Reyal pointed out to him. "Shouldn't we just start yelling for her?"

"Uh, yeah. You're right," Gidley admitted, embarrassed that he had taken the wrong action. Again!

At that moment, Casha brushed past both of them and putting her hands up to her mouth, yelled, "Bellina", as loud as she could.

Turning to Gidley and Reyal she said, "She should be back by now. Didn't you notice she hadn't returned, yet? Start yelling for her."

Gidley and Reyal jumped at the sound of her voice, and obeyed her demand.

"Bel-li-naaa", they all screamed, at the top of their lungs.

That brought Dira and Jinto out of the tent and they also started calling for their friend.

After about five minutes, they all got a sick feeling in the pit of their stomachs. Where could she be? It didn't appear to be a very big forest so she couldn't have gotten very far away. Surely, she could hear their voices.

"She must have fallen and hurt herself or got knocked out, running into a branch," Casha said, heading into the woods.

"Wait!" Gidley called. "We must stay together. We don't want to get separated."

"Yeah," Jinto said. "If somethin' bad got her, we don't want to be getting' caught ourselves, like."

"Jinto is right, although I don't think she got caught by anything," Gidley said. "However, we need to make some torches and go looking for her. Casha was probably right in thinking that Bellina got knocked out. We'll have to find her or she could freeze to death out here tonight."

Binding small branches together with vines and then lighting them, gave the search party plenty of light, even though the torches burned quickly.

They made three each and lit one at a time as they walked together into the forest calling for Bellina every few minutes.

It was difficult for them. They were slipping and running into low branches. Jinto nearly knocked himself out, twice. The brambles that grew there tore at their clothes, and they spent many precious seconds untangling their cloaks. Casha fell a few times and so did Reyal.

After an hour, they were frozen, wet and exhausted. Casha had completely lost her voice, from screaming Bellina's name and all of them were so tired, they feared they couldn't make it back, to the tent. Those woods were larger than they had first thought.

Stopping long enough to get a sip of vita, to rejuvenate themselves, they began circling back, toward the tent.

Bellina had vanished.

Gidley made the decision to get the rest of them back to the safety of the tent, where they could build a fire before they all got sick or froze to death. They were a long way from any other shelter or help.

Reluctantly, they all returned to the tent and built a fire. No one could eat.

Casha sobbed, until she fell asleep, that night.

Chapter 19

BACK TO THE BAILI MOUNTAINS

Very early the next morning everyone woke up at about the same time and quickly ate and packed up their belongings.

Leaving everything in the tent, except, except their weapons, the friends stepped outside to a cold, but sunny day.

"We should split-up into two groups," Gidley said. "I'm hoping Bellina got under a fir tree, like we did when we fell into the river"

"Maybe she didn't know where our voices were coming from last night, it being dark and with all the snow," Dira added.

"Yeah, she had her dagger with her and she's smart," Casha said, and then she started to cry.

Gidley went over to her and took her into his arms. Kissing the top of her head and holding her tight, he assured her that they would find Bellina and, to himself, thought, 'even if she's dead'. Tears filled his eyes.

Letting Casha go, he stepped back and wiped his eyes and said, "Come on, let's get our little, lost traveler back."

Gidley and Casha went left, into the forest, and Jinto and Dira went right. Reyal decided to go straight through. That way they could cover more ground, in less time.

More than an hour later they all met at the opposite side, of the woods.

A very dejected group had not found any sign of Bellina. The snow had stopped late last night, so they hoped she wasn't covered over with snow and that they had missed her body. It was as if she had just dropped from sight.

It was at that moment that Jinto noticed that the snow had drifted around some holes heading out, toward the middle, of the field.

"Maybe her, like, went there, to get her bearings and fell, like," he said, pointing in front of them.

Knowing that they needed to see if she was indeed buried in the snow, but afraid to look, the friends hesitated a moment.

"Stay here," Gidley finally said. "If she's out there, I should be the one to go look for her. You've been through enough on my account."

He pushed through the snow about twenty yards before seeing a large, indentation, that looked like maybe Bellina had fallen there.

'What was that glint, in the snow, over there?' Gidley wondered.

He walked over and picked up Bellina's dagger. Apparently, she had been here and dropped it. Luckily the dagger hadn't fallen too deeply into the snow.

"Come here," Gidley called. "I've found her dagger, but no sign of her other than an area that looks like she may have fallen. There aren't any more footprints in the snow from here. It looks like she just flew away."

"You may be right," Casha said, looking up towards the mountains. "Drazils!" she said pointing.

The others got to Casha and Gidley at that moment and all turned toward the west, where Casha pointed. There were, indeed, drazils circling the peaks of the mountains.

"I think it be real clear, like," Jinto said. "Them drazils done took Miss Bellina!"

"We have to go get her," Casha said and turned to Gidley and grabbed his shoulders, shaking him, as she spoke.

"Okay, okay!" Gidley said, taking her by the wrists before she shook him to death.

"I think we should go back to the tent and pick up all the supplies we will need, and go get her," he decided. "However, I must caution you, she may very well be dead at this point. She may have been eaten by those things up there. I just don't know. We have to be brave, no matter what we find, but we must go get her, whether she's dead or alive."

"Of course she's alive," Casha said, pounding him on the chest.

"Take it easy, Casha," he said. "She's my dear friend, too. I hope she's alive, as much as you do, but you must get hold of yourself and expect that you may have to be very strong. She may be dead."

Everyone listened, with sad hearts. What Gidley said was true. And that is what was also on their minds and weighed heavy, on their hearts.

If she were alive, she deserved their best effort at rescue and if not, they knew they had to at least know. And if they could, they needed to try to bring her body back for burial.

They all needed to keep their heads and they needed a plan. A good, solid, plan.

After a short discussion they decided to go back to the tent and pack up everything and head towards the mountains.

They grabbed a quick bite. Gidley warned them that tired, hungry Elves would be worthless, for a rescue. They all drank some vita. It gave them strength and stamina, for the task ahead.

The rescuers started off toward the Baili Mountains.

"Don't there be Moards up there, like?" Jinto asked.

"Yes," Casha answered, "And I have no idea what they may do. We don't have such creatures in Sharrock, but to be travelers and adventurers, you have to meet up with all kinds."

"Mostly they be nice kinds, I think," Jinto said. "The kinds we met already, I mean, not them Moards and drazils. They be the kind what's mean."

"We may all get a chance to try our new skills," Gidley told them.

"I hope we remember our lessons," Reyal added.

"I wish I had felt as good as I do now," Dira said. "I feel I missed a chance to really better myself."

"We be teachin' you everything," Jinto said. "When you be ready, just say."

It took most of the day to reach the base of the mountains just below where they had spotted the drazils that morning. They didn't see any flying around, now, but they had kept aligned with the peak near where the drazils were circling earlier.

They made a rough camp at the base of the mountain. If alive, Bellina might need attention quickly and they wanted a place to tend her. They set up the tent and ate and tried to sleep. It was dark now and they couldn't climb in the dark. They had to wait until morning and they hoped they wouldn't be too late.

Very early the next morning, after very little sleep, they all assembled around the campfire to discuss the plan.

"We can only take a little food and vita. And we had better take only the daggers. We don't know enough about climbing to take anything else. I couldn't manage myself and a sword," Gidley confessed.

"You're right," Dira said. "Casha, do you have Bellina's dagger?"

"Right here. She'll need it," Casha responded, positively.

"Jinto, pull that rope from the tent. We may need it," Gidley told him. "Okay everyone. We climb and do whatever it takes to get Bellina back. Let's go!"

Gidley said this with more enthusiasm than he felt. He had no idea how to defeat the drazils or any Moards they might encounter. Not to mention, scaling a mountain, which he was sure none of them had ever done before. Sharrock had no mountains. Maybe Bellina wasn't even up there.

Bravely, the little band started off a little after daybreak.

Chapter 20

THE MOARDS

Bellina woke up and realized that she hurt all over. She was cold and hungry.

'I wonder what day it is? How long have I been here?' she thought to herself.

Looking around, she realized that she was in a cave or some kind of stone room. The last memory she had was of being dropped on a ledge on the top of a mountain.

"I must have fainted, or got knocked out," she said. "I'd better find out where I am and how I got here. Wherever, *here,*is," she whispered.

She tried to stand and realized that she was tied up, hands and feet. She couldn't stand and looking down, realized that blood stained her shirt and it was torn in several places. Her cloak was under her and it had blood on it, too.

Sitting there trying to figure out what was going on and what she might do about her situation, she suddenly heard voices. She wasn't able to make out what they were saying, but there were a lot of them.

She was in a room with no windows, but there was a doorway to her left. There were torches burning outside the door and they cast a dim light into the room and on her.

She noticed her flute, still in its case, lying near by.

'No dagger,' she thought. 'Of course, they took that away from me. I'm obviously a prisoner. They have tied me up.'

She giggled at her wit and then sobered. This wasn't funny. Somewhere, the thought crept in that she had dropped her dagger long before she was brought here, but everything was fuzzy.

Bellina tried to clear her head, but she just couldn't think. She noticed the smell next.

It was a damp, sort of moldy odor mixed with a faint, stomach turning stench.

"What is making that smell?" she asked the room. "I hope it's not me."

Sniffing, she realized it wasn't her. Not that she smelled too good, but the odor she smelled was feral and rotten. 'Maybe an animal died in here', she rationalized to herself.

Next she wondered, 'who is that talking?'. 'The birds couldn't talk, could they?' she questioned. She wasn't thinking clearly.

"Oh, no," she said softly, as she remembered. "It must be those Moards. What was said about them? What had Mulop told them about Moards? Goblins. He said they were Goblins. Do Goblins eat Elves?"

Bellina started to cry. She was terrified. She then thought of her friends. They must be frantic. They would save her. She realized then, that she had no idea where she was. If she didn't know, how could her friends know?

"I'm cold and scared and hungry," Bellina said, between sobs.

At that moment, a strange creature appeared in the doorway. He was taller than Bellina and he had an ugly, sharp face. His ears were longer than Elf ears and the smell was definitely coming from him. He was very skinny, with long pointy fingers and feet. He had no hair, on his head and he was a funny, sickly, white color, like he never got outside, into the sun.

He looked at her with his tiny, blinking eyes and she felt her heart stop. He walked over to her and poked her, hard.

Bellina let out a yell. He poked her again, this time so hard, she fell over and she cried out, again.

She lay there with her face pressed against the cold, dirty floor. The Moard turned and left. Bellina tried to get off her arm, so she could move her face back on to her cloak. After much trying, she succeeded. She lay there crying, until she fell asleep.

Grac left the room and joined the others.

"She's scared, but I think she is okay," he reported.

"We should kill her now and have her for our dinner," Lork said. "I'm hungry."

"No," Grac replied. "We can't kill her. Not yet. We must find out why those Elves are seeking us."

"We know why. They have discovered our secret," Lork said, angrily. "They know and they want to destroy us. I saw the Elf from Thorpeshire helping them. They have trained for battle. They seek us! All the Elves are gathering and they seek us!"

At that moment, Erck ran into the room, "They come toward the mountain. The Elves!"

"Hurry, get the prisoner and take her far below. Prepare for battle," Grac shouted.

The Moards scrambled to do as he said. They had lived in these mountains for many years, after what they called the Great War of Bloodshed. They had banded together, fifty of them, and broken away from the Goblin colony of Drog, north, in the Magenta Mountains. They had settled here. The war was long fought and over, many years ago and they set up a new colony. They called it Yanog and they mined the old, abandoned tunnels of the Dwarves, who had moved eastward.

That's where the Moards had discovered a small vein of the rare gem, kimbar. The first ones ever found in the Baili Mountains.

They knew the Elves had found out, somehow, and now came to claim the gems for themselves. Soon the Dwarves and Fairies would come. The other Elves from Thorpeshire and Sanadula and Dordom would come.

Already, Elves from Thorpeshire, were trying to discover where they were. And the Elves from Dordom were overheard asking about kimbar gems. They were heard talking about how rich they would become.

Yes, the Moards saw and heard enough to know that they had to prepare to defend their treasure. Now, they had the Elf spy. They would force her to tell them everything.

Even now the other Elves began to climb the mountain.

"We will defend what is ours," Grac swore.

Three Moards grabbed Bellina and roughly, half dragged, half carried her deep into the mountain tunnels. When she cried out, one of them hit her hard across the back and told her to shut up. He tied a foul smelling cloth, across her mouth.

She was dumped on the cold, damp floor and her cloak was thrown on the floor near her. They tossed her flute down, hitting her on the head. She was left alone in the dark prison room.

Bellina being dragged by Moards

Chapter 21

UP THE MOUNTAIN

After several hours of climbing and almost as much sliding back down, the group of rescuers had reached nearly half way up the section of mountain, where they had seen the drazils circling the day before.

"My hands be pretty sore, like," Jinto lamented, when they took a much needed break.

"I have blisters and scrapes, on places I don't even have body," Casha sighed.

Her companions laughed, at her unintentional humor. It was the first laughter from any of them, since Bellina went missing.

Casha smiled, "I'm so glad my pain is so amusing."

"Casha, you know we are teasing you. We don't want you to be in pain," Reyal laughed.

Gidley walked over and gently taking her hand, raised it up to his lips and kissed the blisters on her fingers.

"They should be all better, now," he said. "But you should put something on them and then, put your gloves on."

"Ooh," Jinto, Dira and Reyal said.

Casha pulled her hand away. Blushing, she thanked Gidley for his concern. And to the others she said, "Mind your business!"

Thus chided, the other three busied themselves checking their bundles.

Casha turned to Gidley and smiled, "It's going to be alright, isn't it?"

"About Bellina? Uh, ye, yeah, sure," Gidley stuttered.

'It has to be,' he thought. 'I could never forgive myself, if something happened to her. I couldn't live with myself."

"You don't sound sure," Casha challenged him. "You're the leader. You should sound more positive. You should encourage us."

"Casha, please. I don't know. She may not even be up there. I feel responsible, I feel awful and she's my friend too! I just don't know. I'm in over my head," Gidley said, pleading with her for understanding.

"You're right. I'm sorry. I guess I'm just emotional. So much has happened to us all and now Bellina. She's like a sister. I...," Casha began.

"She's like a sister to me, too. Don't forget that. I never wanted anything to happen to any of you, any of my friends. Casha, I love you and not like a sister," Gidley confessed.

"I know, Gidley. I love you, too," She said gently. "Let's go get Bellina. We can do it!"

They climbed, Gidley first, then Casha. Next came Dira and Reyal. Jinto brought up the rear.

They were doing quite well and making good time in spite of none of them knowing what they were doing. Then they reached a portion of the mountain that was one huge boulder, nine feet tall and very smooth. Gidley got about four feet up and couldn't find any holds to pull himself up the rest of the way. He told Casha and they began to back down.

The group surveyed their options. They could go back down, about thirty feet and start over; no one wanted that, or they could move to the right, around the boulder and resume the climb. The problem, with that plan, was that the only way over to an easier climb up, was over a *six-inch wide ledge*.

Elves are very nimble so, of course, they chose to move by way of the ledge.

"We'd better use the rope to tie ourselves together, just in case," Gidley suggested.

"Good Idea," Casha said.

Dira passed the end of the rope to her and she handed it to Gidley. He tied it around his waist and each one, in line, did the same.

When they were done, Gidley stepped out onto the narrow ledge. He faced the rock wall and held on, but the face of the rock was so smooth that he just used the rock to lean against, as he inched forward. There were no handholds.

Gidley had made his way, about fifteen feet, when Dira stepped onto a portion of the ledge that gave away beneath his feet.

It happened so quickly, that he startled Casha and pulled her back, almost sending her tumbling off the mountain.

Reyal saw Dira start to fall and he braced himself, the best he could. Jinto immediately braced himself, too. They saved Dira from falling down the mountain, and possibly, taking all of them with him.

When Casha slipped, Gidley was jerked back and he almost fell. Luckily there was a small stone outcrop and he grabbed it and held on. That saved Casha from falling too far, although she dangled from the rope, one hand desperately holding what was left of the ledge. She managed to get her foot onto a rock and pushed herself upwards. Gidley reached down, as far as he could and helped pull her up. Dira, on the other end of Casha's part of the rope, also pulled at the same time. There was enough leverage for her to get back up onto the ledge.

Shaken, but okay, Dira stepped over the broken portion of the ledge. Reyal and Jinto followed carefully behind.

Another five feet and Gidley stepped onto a wide shelf and saw an easier climb before him. Once everyone had made it onto the shelf, Gidley started climbing again.

Casha was breathing funny, but insisted she was fine and followed him up.

About twenty-five feet from the top, the climbers faced their most terrifying moments. A drazil screamed it's awful sound, as it dove and tried to pick Gidley off the face of the mountain. Luckily he had a firm footing and he was able to hold on with one hand and pull out his dagger, with the other one. As it struck, Gidley stabbed upwards and caught the drazil in the neck. It let out an earsplitting scream and plunged down the side of the mountain.

Two more dove, at the group.

Bracing themselves and getting the best handholds that they could, each climber pulled out their dagger just, as soon as Gidley started his fight with the first drazil. They were ready when the attack came.

Reyal stabbed at one drazil's foot, while Dira, who was above him, thrust his dagger into its belly. It too, screamed and fell down the mountain.

Casha was stabbing at a third drazil and almost dropped her dagger. Dira was able to reach upwards and stab into the drazil, but could not kill it. He was too far below it and at an awkward angle.

Bleeding, but still able to fly, the drazil wheeled around and came at Jinto. He and Reyal reached out, at the same time, and stabbed the drazil, who then joined the others at the bottom of the mountain.

The group was shaken up, but couldn't take time to check for wounds. The drazils had alerted the Moards, who at that very moment were preparing for battle.

Gidley reached another wide ledge, just as the first Moards entered the tunnel and started upwards.

Gidley had just climbed onto the upper-most ledge in front of the tunnel and was helping Casha up, when the Moards appeared.

Gidley pulled off the rope and turned to fight for his life.

Casha pulled herself up over the top and quickly untied the rope from her waist and joined Gidley in battle.

There were only three Moards, so far, but Gidley and Casha suspected there were lots more inside.

Dira was now up and joined the battle, then came Reyal and Jinto, their daggers in hand.

They were too much for the first three Moards, who were quickly slain.

The five friends advanced toward the tunnel. Their hearts almost stopped. There were at least fifteen more Moards coming up the narrow passageway.

They braced themselves for the fight.

Using their sword fighting footwork and being faster and apparently better trained than their opponents, the group had already killed several Moards, when the leader stopped and said, "We can't win against those trained by the Dwarves. Go back and get better weapons."

They all turned and ran back down the tunnel.

Trying to catch their breath, the group looked at each other in bewilderment.

"They be a strange bunch, them do," Jinto said.

"Why did they run away?" Reyal asked. "This is rather puzzling."

"I believe the leader said they were getting other weapons," Gidley answered. "We could be in serious trouble."

"We have to get Bellina," Casha reminded them. "I'm sure those things have her."

"Don't worry. We haven't forgotten why we are here," Dira said. "I think Gidley's right, though. We had better start down there and fight the best we can. It may be hopeless, but we've got to try. We are Bellina's only hope. If she's still alive."

"She's alive!" Casha said sharply.

"Let's go then," Gidley said, leading them forward.

Chapter 22

THE RESCUE

Bellina stirred. She had apparently fallen asleep. Where was everyone?

'I'm so hungry and thirsty' she thought and realized that she had the cloth still tied around her mouth. Bellina tried to sit up.

It took a few tries, but she finally made it. She reached up and pulled the dirty rag away from her mouth and sat holding her head in her hands. Her hands were getting numb from the ties binding her wrists, and her ankles hurt from the leather thong tying her feet together. Her head hurt.

At that moment, someone came into the room holding a candle. The light seemed very bright, after the complete darkness of her prison room and it hurt her eyes. She couldn't tell who was standing there.

Hopeful that she was being rescued she called out," Gidley, Casha?

"Who is Gidleycasha?" asked a rough voice.

'Oh, no,' thought Bellina, 'it's one of those awful Moards.'

"Well? Who is Gidleycasha," he asked again. "Is he the Elf, who tries to rescue you? Is he the one who leads the Elves in the fight? The one who kills my friends, the one who wants to steal our jewels. Answer me, spy."

"Steal what jewels? Who is a spy?" asked Bellina, confused, by the line of questioning.

He made it sound like Gidley and her friends were at fault for some reason, when it was the Moards, clearly, who had kidnapped *her*.

"We know you seek our jewels," the Moard said. "We know you have trained with the best Dwarf, in the use of bows and arrows and trained with the best Gnome, in the art of sword fighting. We know the Elves of Thorpeshire and Dordom are helping you. What we need to know is the full plan. You must tell us or die."

"What are you talking about?" Bellina asked, very perplexed. None of what he said made any sense. "You think we are seeking you? We seek *The Dagger of Bahyel*, stolen from my friend Gidley. I don't know who you are or why you have taken me prisoner. My friends come here only to save me. I promise you, we weren't even headed this way. We were going to Fala, in the Realm of Delightment."

"You lie! You want the jewels," he insisted. "You must give up information or you die."

Bellina said, in a strong voice, "I need water and food or I'll die anyway and I won't tell you anything."

"I'll get water," he said, and was gone.

Bellina was more puzzled than ever. Were they harmful, or were they just confused about having to defend their jewels? Was this all a big mistake? It dawned on her that if they were miners in these tunnels, they must have discovered jewels, as he had said. But why do they think we want them?

Someone entered and gave Bellina a cup of water. It was warm and tasted funny, but it was wet and Bellina needed it badly. She gulped it down.

"Thank you," Bellina said.

The Moard just took the cup back and started out of the room without a word, then, he stopped and came back. He picked Bellina's cloak up from the floor and brought it over to her.

"Thank you," she said, again.

The Moard, then handed her the flute.

"Could I have my hands free, so I may play? My feet are bound and I don't know where I am, so I can't get away," she begged.

"Amuse yourself, with your toy," the Moard told her, as he untied her hands. "Someone will come and question you soon. If you refuse to help us, you will die. Already your friends have killed many of our group. Grac is right now, getting more weapons ready. We will defeat your friends. They will never get you."

The Moard left and Bellina was filled with hope at his words. Casha and Gidley had already come for her. Wonderful Jinto, Dira and Reyal were fighting the Moards and coming for her.

She was so lifted by this news that she forgot her hunger and pain. She lifted her flute and began to play. The magical sound filled the room and spilled out the door.

Bellina didn't know it, but a very curious thing happened. The Moards, preparing swords and bows and arrows with the intention of killing all of the group of trespassing Elves, including Bellina, suddenly stopped what they were doing and listened to the music.

Meanwhile, Gidley and the rest of the group wandered down one tunnel, after another. They had no idea how to get to the Moards and they hadn't come across Bellina yet, either.

Dira, who was getting tired of wandering around, in the dark suggested they just sit and wait for the Moards to come back and fight.

"Don't be ridiculous!" Casha retorted. "We have to find them and kill them or find Bellina and get out of here."

"But, if they be gettin' other weapons, like, don't they be killin' us?" Jinto asked.

"What kind of weapons do Moards have," Reyal asked.

No one knew the answers to their questions.

"Let's go," Gidley said. "We won't find out anything sitting here."

They wandered around for another twenty minutes or so, when Jinto observed, "They be havin' a bad time gettin' their weapons, like. Shouldn't we be fightin' 'em by now?"

"Jinto's right," Casha said. "They should have found *us* by now even if we can't find them!"

"Shh," Gidley said. "I hear music."

"Do you think they be havin' a party?" Jinto asked, in amazement.

"I doubt a party," Gidley said, "but, I think I hear a sweet, sounding flute."

"Bellina!" they all said, at once.

Gidley listened for a few minutes more and said, "It's coming from that tunnel, on the left."

"Yes, I hear it plainly from that tunnel," Reyal agreed.

They all made their way, in the darkness, toward the tunnel Gidley had indicated. After a few yards down the tunnel it turned sharply to the right and once they had gone around the bend, they could all hear the golden notes floating up to them.

"She be magic on that flute," Jinto said.

The group saw a light ahead and quickly made their way down the last passage and into a large room carved out of the rock.

More than magic. They were startled to come upon the Moards, who were standing around or sitting and listening to Bellina play the flute. They weren't getting their weapons ready and they didn't acknowledge that the rescuers had entered, what was obviously the meeting room!

Casha yelled out, " Bellina, its Casha! Don't stop playing. We'll get you in a few moments."

"Wow, that flute *is* magic," Gidley exclaimed. "It doesn't work on us, except to calm us, but it apparently works on our enemies."

"Great, but let's get Bellina and get out of here," Reyal urged them.

Jinto and Dira grabbed several torches and led the way to where Bellina played for her life.

Casha began to cry when she saw her dear friend, bruised and bleeding, with her feet bound. Bellina was tired and dirty and playing the flute that she could barely hold up to her lips.

Jinto handed his torch, to Gidley and bent down and scooped Bellina up while Casha tucked the cape around her. Casha gave her a sip of vita, as Reyal took the flute and began to play. The magic held and Jinto turned with his precious bundle and left the prison room.

Gidley said to Reyal, "Keep playing until the others get up the tunnel, we'll stay behind. Once they get far enough up the tunnel, we'll follow. The Moards will most likely come out of their trance, because they won't be able to hear the music anymore. They will come after us, so you'll have to play each time they get close enough to hear."

Reyal nodded and kept playing. He wondered how he was going to climb down the mountain and play at the same time. That's if they were even able to find their way back out.

A few minutes later, Dira came back into the room.

"Gidley, great news," Dira said excitedly, "We were going back up the tunnel and this time, with the torches, we could see another tunnel off to the right. Casha said she thought I should go see if it led anywhere. I ran down and the tunnel took a sharp turn and I could see light. I checked and it leads outside, about thirty feet from the bottom of the mountain. We seem to be a ways from the tent, but we don't have to climb all the way back down. It's getting dark, though, so we'd better hurry."

"Boy, we sure are lucky," Gidley said, with relief.

Reyal played and nodded.

They hurried from the room and ran up the tunnel, as fast as they could go. Dira led the way to the new passage and outside.

UNEASY TRUCE

Once outside, Gidley quickly informed them of his plan. They were all to start down the mountain and make their way to the tent. Everyone, except Bellina, should start packing everything up immediately.

"We will travel by night, for a while, until we get away from here. Hurry! Reyal can't play forever," Gidley said. "How are you Bellina?"

"Much better. Casha gave me more vita and some fruit," Bellina explained. "I'm tired and sore, but I can make it back to the tent."

"I be carrying you back, if walking be too hard, ma'am," Jinto assured her.

"Uh, oh!" Gidley said. "I hear our friends."

"Get going everyone." Dira urged them

Reyal put the flute, to his lips, ready to play.

"Wait a minute," Casha said. "How are you and Reyal supposed to get away? He can't climb down and play the flute at the same time. Each time he stops our little buddies will be all over you. They'll follow you to the tent, even if you can make it that far. We can't get away."

As she finished, the Moards came streaming down the tunnel. Reyal began to play and they stopped where they stood, a smile on their ugly faces.

"Casha is right, as usual," Gidley exclaimed. 'I never think things through. Every time I feel like I'm getting the hang, of this leadership thing, something comes along to remind me that I'm in over my head,' he told himself.

"Okay, Casha take Bellina down to the tent. Try to get as much packed up as possible. We'll be there, as soon as, we finish up here," Gidley told them.

"Oh, no! I'm not leaving, now. I can fight, as good as, anybody else. I'm staying!" Casha informed him.

"Well, we could kill them while they are in the trance," Dira offered.

"I can't believe you said that," Gidley said astonished and looked at Dira. "We can't kill them in cold blood. We have to fight them!"

With that, Gidley told Reyal to give the flute back to Bellina and draw his dagger.

The Moards began advancing, once again.

The friends all drew their daggers and stood ready for the battle.

The first Moard reached Jinto, who stepped forward and swung his arm at the same time. This gave him leverage and he easily stabbed his foe.

One Moard ran up to Gidley and slashing down, cut Gidley's arm. Startled at the pain that burned quickly and then stopped hurting right away, Gidley stabbed at his attacker just as a second Moard rushed up to him.

Dira stepped from behind and helped Gidley fight off the two Moards.

Casha made a sword fighting motion, with her dagger and when the Moard coming after her swung his sword, she swung her dagger up and connected with his arm. His sword fell useless at his feet. As he stood in bewilderment, Casha stepped forward and punched him hard, on the nose. He fell into a deep sleep at her feet. A second Moard, who ran up at the same time, also got punched. Before he knew what hit him, he also landed next to his fellow Moard at her feet.

Casha was very satisfied that she was able to knock them out instead of having to kill them.

'This gold ring from Queen Findra may not be magic, but it sure has made it easy to knock people out', she thought. 'It also seems to work on lupodes, if I remember correctly!'

Reyal had three Moards jabbing at him. He killed one and just as he drew back his dagger for another strike, he was slashed on the forearm with a sword.

Bellina began to play her flute.

The fight stopped immediately.

Fighting the Moards

Several Moards were dead or knocked out and Gidley and Reyal were bleeding badly. Casha gave them both some vita and tearing pieces from her shirt, bound their wounds.

Dira had a cut on his cheek, but it wasn't deep. Jinto had a few cuts on his hands, but he wasn't in trouble.

This is ridiculous! We are outnumbered and only have these stupid daggers," Gidley cried. "What are we going to do?"

"I don't see much use in continuing like this," Reyal said. "I mean, we can kill just so many and then stop them with the music. Why not just kill them all, now. And before you say, 'we can't kill them, in cold blood', if we stop every time we get into trouble, isn't that the same thing? We do have the advantage, even if we are outnumbered."

"You're right. I'll try talking to them," Gidley answered. "As soon as Bellina stops playing, I'll yell to them and we'll see what happens. If they'll let us go, we'll just go. Otherwise, I'm afraid we'll have to do the best we can with Bellina stopping the fight when we get overpowered. I, at least, think we should give them a chance to end this. I'm sorry, Reyal, but I don't know any other way to do this. We have the magic flute for our protection and advantage, so I guess we should use it. Does anyone have a problem with this or disagree?"

They all said, 'No'.

"Okay, I guess I'll try talking to them. Is everyone ready?"

"Yes," they all said, and Bellina stopped playing.

Before the Moards could move, Casha shouted, "Stop! You must listen to me. Sorry, Gidley, but I have the power of reasoning."

Gidley stood with his mouth open to speak, but just nodded to Casha.

Stepping forward she continued, "Your men are dying. We are fast and well trained and have skills you and your men do not possess. We also have magic and reasoning. You cannot win. Our magic flute will stop you anytime Bellina plays it. If we feel we are losing this battle, we will stop you and kill you all while you sit and wait for us to do it. Tell us what you want from us and we may be able to come to a truce."

"You are here to steal our jewels," Grac told her. "We can't let you do that. They are ours and we need them to survive. We will fight to our death to defend what belongs to us."

"What jewels?" Gidley asked. "We only came here because you kidnapped our friend. We want to leave. We have an important mission. Our Queen Findra has sent us to retrieve *The Dagger of Bahyel*, stolen, from me. It is our kingdom's most priceless treasure."

"You trained with the Dwarves to learn skills to defeat us," Grac continued. "We have seen you with Elves of other realms, making plans to steal our gems. Somehow, you have found out our secret."

"I have no idea what you are talking about," Gidley said in frustration.

"We did train, but that's because the Elves we seek are very bad and not only have stolen my dagger, but they have stolen from others and have killed an Elf, just because they didn't like how *he* spoke to them. We had no fighting skills and the Elf who helped us when we were attacked by your drazils, also helped us find the Dwarf who trained us. But, he trained us with the bow and arrow and the Gnome trained us with the sword. As you can see, we only have daggers. If we were trying to kill you and steal your jewels, we could have done a better job than this with our other weapons."

Gidley didn't mention that the only reason they only had daggers was because of the climb up the mountain. They didn't need to know that, however.

"Are you taking your friend and leaving?" Grac asked them.

"Bellina is all we wanted," Casha answered. "We don't know about any gems. We need to go before the dagger we seek disappears forever. The dagger has many rare gems on the hilt and we are afraid the thieves will remove the stones and destroy the dagger. As Gidley has already told you, it is a priceless treasure to us, just as your gems are priceless, to you. The gems in our dagger are the very rare stone, kimbar. There is no way we or anyone else could ever replace them. Our Queen may never let us go home again, if we fail in our quest."

"We be wantin' to leave, like, if you don't mind. We all want to get back home, where there are no bad people and drazils and such," Jinto added.

Grac was clearly upset and it looked as if he wanted to believe them, but didn't quite trust them.

"Okay, we'll retreat into this tunnel," Grac finally said. "You leave and we won't harm you. We fear your magic and your fighting skills. Some of my friends have been killed, but I warn you; if you don't leave, we will fight until there is no one left. You or us, it doesn't matter. If we are dead, we will have no use for the gems."

"What kind of gems do you have?" Bellina asked. "I'd like to know what you have that's so valuable and so important to you that you would kidnap and almost kill me, and attack my friends and risk your own life and the lives of your friends? What is that important? I don't understand."

"Kimbars! Shouted Lork, stepping, from behind Grac. "We have found kimbars. The Baili Mountains have been good to us. It has given us her secret. We know you found out, because we heard Elves talking about them. The Dordom Elves. I heard them myself."

"The Dordom Elves are the ones who have our dagger," Gidley tried again. "Our dagger has kimbars on the hilt. Haven't you been listening? They were talking about *our* kimbars, not yours. We've just killed a bunch of you for nothing, not to mention what you put Bellina through and Casha. All of us have been worried sick and we have lost time. All for nothing. It was all for nothing. We're leaving, you make me sick."

Gidley turned his back on the Moards and walked towards the edge of the mountain.

"Come on, let's get out of here," he said.

They all turned and followed him back down the mountain and they soon arrived at the tent. The Moards didn't follow them.

Once they were back at the tent, Casha threw her arms around Gidley and told him how proud she was of him. In turn they all came up and shook his hand and hugged him.

"You were so brave," Bellina said hugging him. "Thank you, for rescuing me."

"I be pleased, to travel with you," Jinto said, hugging him so tight, he almost passed out.

Reyal offered him his hand and then hugged him, too.

Dira, embarrassed, just shook his hand, then decided he had better hug him.

Gidley laughed and thanked everyone for sticking with him.

They all decided that since it was so late and they were all either hurt or exhausted or both, that they couldn't go on.

They also decided that they should take turns keeping watch, all night, in case the Moards were planning a nighttime ambush.

Dira volunteered to take the first watch.

Casha and Jinto, tended their friends wounds by applying the ointment they had gotten from Mulop.

Casha bathed and fed Bellina, then wrapped her in a blanket and held her until she fell into a deep asleep.

Luckily, the night passed quietly.

Chapter 21

THE BAILI MOUNTAINS TREASURE

The sun was shining brightly the next morning and everyone went about packing up their belongings.

Jinto finished first and stood outside staring up at the mountains. Two drazils were circling the highest peak, but were a ways off from the campsite. Jinto kept an eye on them for a while and when it became apparent that neither they, nor the Moards were paying them any attention, he relaxed and wandered over towards the base, of the mountain.

He was noticing some interesting stones, with a squared off shape and he thought how useful they would be, in wall building.

Something glinted in the sun and he wondered what it was.

' Maybe someone lost something valuable,' he thought, and he strolled over, to have a close look.

Jinto was a simple man, with plain tastes and very little by way of possessions, but he realized that the shine in the sun was something very beautiful and probably worth a good deal of money. Where a section of the mountain had broken off, probably during a storm, was a section of rock that glittered with a bright yellow glow.

"Them be kimbar, I'll bet my life," he said and called to his friends, to come out immediately.

They all rushed out for his excitement sounded like danger was near.

They were relieved to find that he just wanted them to see something he had found.

They all stared wide-eyed, when Gidley, who was the only one to ever see kimbars up close, proclaimed that they probably were the rare, kimbar gem. It was hard to tell because they were still rough, on the rock, which grew them.

"Might we be taking some?" Jinto asked.

"Oh, yes," Gidley said smiling. "We will be taking some. We may need them, after our adventure is over and Queen Findra makes us leave Sharrock."

"Oh, Gidley," Casha chided him. "You sound so negative. We'll find those Elves and get your dagger back. Now, let's get some gems. I think this mountain owes us."

"Won't we be breaking our promise, to them Moards," Jinto wanted to know.

"Why?" Reyal asked. "We didn't steal anything, from them. If they knew these were here, they would have gotten them already."

"Yeah, this is finders-keepers," Dira added.

Using their daggers, the friends dug out, as many kimbars as they were able, since they didn't possess the proper tools, to break the rock open.

"I wish we had a pick-axe," Reyal commented. "I'll be happy with what I got, but I wish we could see if this is a vein or just a small crystal rock."

"There are a lot of stones here and easy to dig out, even without proper tools," Dira said. "Once these are cut and polished, they will make us rich."

Gidley looked over at Bellina. She wasn't getting any stones.

"What's wrong, Bellina? Gidley called to her. "Don't feel able to dig out any stones?'

"No, I guess I hurt more that I thought," she answered. "I have a few. It will be more than enough. I don't need wealth."

"Here, have some of mine," Casha told her, letting the golden gems fall into her friend's hand.

"Sure," Gidley said. "I have plenty, too. Take these."

"Why don't we just divide these equally among us," Reyal suggested. "We're all in this together."

"We should see what Jinto wants to do," Gidley said. "After all, he found them."

"It be okay to divide 'em, like," Jinto said. "I called you all out, so we could share in the treasure. I'll not be takin' more than my share. We will divide 'em equal, like. You'd be doin' the same, if it be any of you, what found 'em."

"Thanks to you, Jinto we'll all have a good life," Gidley said.

"Thanks to all of you, I be already be havin' a good life," Jinto answered.

Once they had gotten all the gems they could easily pry out, they did divide them equally and all were happy and in a good mood for the day's travel.

The friends finished packing their belongings and started on their way.

They talked excitedly for many miles, about the treasure they had found.

"Yep, them Baili Mountains owed us," Jinto echoed Casha's earlier thought

They all agreed and laughed.

They stopped for lunch and rested a while. No one was tired, but Bellina was having a hard time keeping up and she didn't want to complain. They all realized that she was being very brave, but she had been through a lot, alone, and they knew she didn't feel very good today.

Casha had offered to braid her hair before they left the campsite this morning, but Bellina said it was okay to just tie a string around it. That worried Casha, because Bellina always took pride in her appearance and always braided her hair every morning.

'I had better keep an eye on her,' Casha thought to herself.

Before they resumed the day's travel, Casha changed the dressing on Gidley's and Reyal's arms and washed Dira's face where he got cut, during the fight. Thankfully, no one had been cut, too deeply. They didn't seem aware of their wounds, which she took as a good sign.

After checking the map, Gidley was ready to lead the little group to Fala, in the Realm of Delightment.

They all looked forward to nice, soft, warm beds and a good bath and meal. They couldn't get to Fala fast enough.

Reyal played the flute to ease their walking, as Bellina showed no interest in playing. The magic flute that had saved all their lives, hung useless from her belt.

By late afternoon they had traveled almost to Fala. Even with Bellina not feeling well and walking slower than usual, they had made good time.

They were all surprised when Gidley held up his hand and said, "Shh"

"I'm really starting to hate it when you do that," Casha complained. "Every time, we end up in trouble."

"I hear voices," was all Gidley said.

"Do they be good voices, like or bad?" Jinto wanted to know.

Gidley laughed, "I don't know, Jinto. I just hear things. I don't predict if it's trouble."

"Well, if they're talking, I guess it's not lupodes or drazils, this time," Casha said.

"I smell smoke," Dira added.

"Must be coming from that campfire," Gidley said, pointing ahead.

"Hello," he called to the two Elves, who sat by the fire.

The Elves looked up and said, "Hello, travelers, come join our fire and tell us how you come to be here."

"Why?" Reyal asked. "Aren't we supposed to be here? Are we on your land?"

"Oh, no!" the first Elf said. "I meant it in a friendly way. You don't look like thieves or evil beings. It isn't often we find other Elves traveling here. This land belongs to the Fairies."

"I'm Gidley and these are my friends and we are traveling to Fala for rest and food. We have had a long and dangerous journey. We have just left the Moards, where we had a battle. They had taken Bellina prisoner," Gidley informed them, pointing to Bellina, who managed a half smile.

She walked over near the fire and sat down.

"I'm Bellina," she said.

"I am Adone, this is my brother, Samal," Adone told them.

Adone was about four feet tall with straight, light brown hair and brown eyes. He was slim and muscular and had a quiet, seriousness about him. They could tell that he was probably the older of the two, because he seemed more commanding.

Samal was shorter, by about an inch, with the same brown hair and eyes of his brother and he had the most engaging smile and friendly laugh. His whole face lit up when he smiled, with a hidden mischief.

They were both very pleasant to look at.

"They are Jinto, Dira, Reyal and Casha," Gidley said, pointing out each of the friends, not introduced already. We come from Sharrock, in the south.

"I know where it is," Adone said. "We are from Thorpeshire, just south of the Baili Mountains. We are also going to Fala. May we join together in the journey?"

"Sure," Bellina said, before anyone could say anything else.

"We would be honored to travel with you," Gidley said, shooting a strange look at Bellina.

"What is your business in Fala?" Samal asked. "If you may say. We go to see the Queen. We are worried about Prince Nekop of Dordom. We need to find out if Queen Zerena has heard of any problems and to warn her, if she has not. Our brother has been on a scouting mission and his report was one of possible trouble. There is unease and rumblings from our neighbors in Dordom.

"We are only going to Fala for rest, as I said," Gidley explained. "We seek evil Elves from Dordom, who have stolen a priceless dagger from me. We have been charged by our Queen to get this dagger back, at all costs."

"Hmm. I'll guess then that you are the travelers my brother, Dash, helped," Adone said.

"Yes, yes, it is us! Dash had become a good friend and traveling companion. We were sad to have to leave him," an excited Reyal, told them.

"Yes," the others all agreed.

'Oh, I knew I liked the looks of these two,' Bellina thought, smiling. 'They reminded me of Dash.'

Chapter 25

AUDIENCE WITH THE QUEEN

The group of new friends and old friends quickly became all friends, as they sat and ate and traded stories about their adventures. Bellina even played a song for them.

Gidley realized as they spoke, that Adone and Samal and Dash had been adventuring and training all their lives, while he and his friends could only relate tales from this, their first and only adventure.

But what an adventure it was! Hearing Adone and Samal asking questions and showing amazement at some of their exploits, Gidley started to feel that they really were having a great adventure. Surely, it rivaled things that Adone and Samal had spoken of. He felt like a true leader. He began to realize that he had brought all six of them through much peril and many hardships. The injuries they suffered were painful, but they weren't life threatening. They had managed to get out of all the problems that had befallen them with a little bit of co-operation on everyone's part and the use of all their new found skills. They made a good team.

Gidley knew that it was a group effort and without the others he would have given up long ago or gotten himself killed.

"We couldn't have done it without Gidley leading us," Dira was saying.

"He be a true hero," Jinto added.

Everyone agreed.

Gidley blushed and said, "Thanks, but you know I messed up and I'm not a good leader. You are just good, loyal friends. We have all contributed to our adventures and traveled hard."

"Look, take the compliments and don't be so hard on yourself. You guys have had an amazing time. Enjoy the good parts, while you can, and learn from your mistakes," Samal told him.

"Let's get some sleep," Adone said. "We have a long day ahead of us."

The following morning they started out early. Apparently, Adone and Samal were morning people. Very, early, morning people.

The others were not. They wandered around trying to get packed up. As the group started walking, they had a hard time seeing where they were going.

Adone and Samal teased them and made jokes, but they were too sleepy to care.

Since Adone and Samal had ponies, they offered Casha and Bellina a ride, while they would walk and lead the ponies. Both girls gratefully accepted.

At nine o'clock, they stopped for breakfast.

Casha wanted to change Gidley's and Reyal's dressings, but Samal had some herbal salve and he took care of the dressing of their wounds today.

By the time Samal was done, and as they ate, most of them were fully awake and asked questions about the town of Fala, the Fairies who lived there and Queen Zerena.

They were happy to learn that they would be there by suppertime and that the Fairies were very nice and had wonderful magical powers. Queen Zerena, they learned, was very beautiful and kind and was a much loved and respected ruler.

When they asked about the crystal palace, both Samal and Adone told them that words could not describe it and they would have to be patient and wait to see it for themselves.

Encouraged by this news and eager to see the palace, everyone was rested, full, and anxious to get to Fala.

As they continued on their journey the travelers were surprised to find the snow was less here than everywhere else that they had been.

"Why do they have less snow?" Bellina asked. "Shouldn't they have more snow, being further north?"

"Oh, no," said Samal laughing, "Delightment is surrounded by mountains and the Fairies have some kind of magical aura over the entire area. As we get closer to Fala, you shouldn't see any snow and there probably will be flowers blooming. It's like springtime, all year, there."

And indeed he was right, because a few hours later it got warmer, the snow was gone and it did indeed seem like springtime. There was a cloudless sky of bright blue, birds were singing in leaf-covered trees and flowers bloomed, everywhere.

This was a welcome sight for Bellina, who still suffered the ill effects from her rough treatment by the Moards. She wasn't still hurting, but she had been so frightened and she found it hard to get rid of the memory of the smell and ill treatment.

The warm sun and cool, fragrant breezes made her feel better. In fact, she felt so much better she opted to walk for a while and she even played her flute, which made her feel even better and also cheered her friends. They had been so worried about her.

They began to see their first Fairies flying around, gathering flowers. They stopped to wave at the travelers.

The group removed their cloaks and the woolen shirts, leaving on only their undershirts. Soon they removed their leather boots, as it became too warm to be dressed in their winter garb.

Finally, they reached the lovely city of Fala. The magnificent gold and crystal palace could be seen glittering in the distance, but it was breathtaking, when they arrived and stood before it. It glowed in the sun like a wonderful jewel and they were all awestruck.

Several Fairies flew down and hovered near them.

"Hail, strangers," the first Fairy said.

"Hello," the travelers all said, together.

"May we help you? Do you need directions?" asked a second Fairy.

"I am Adone and this is my brother, Samal. We come from Thorpeshire and are here to see Queen Zerena.

"And you?" asked the first Fairy, turning to the rest of the group.

"I am Gidley, these are my friends. We are from Sharrock. We also would like to see your Queen."

"I am Ena. Wait one moment and I will tell the Queen you are here." She flew off towards the palace.

A few moments later, she was back and said, "Queen Zerena would love to have you all come to see her."

"You must come, now. We will give you food and rest. I am Lea," said the second Fairy. "Let us know if there is anything you need while you are here."

They followed the two Fairies, who directed them to stand near the palace.

"Wait right here," said Lea, pointing to her left. "The Queen will appear on that balcony and speak with you."

The palace stood about five feet tall and was approximately five feet wide and seven feet long, with towers and turrets. It looked like it had been carved out of ice. They knew that it was actually crystal, as Mrs. Baloc had told them a good deal about what it would look like. They still could not believe it, even as they stood before it, and had no doubt why all the Kings and Queens wished they could have one of their own.

At that moment, the Queen stepped out onto the small balcony, at eye level, with her visitors.

She was beautiful and very regal, even though she was only six inches tall. She had long blond hair and pale, almost icy, blue eyes. She was dressed in a silver gown, and wore a silver crown studded with diamonds, on her head.

All of this pale, almost absence of color, should have been cold and forbidding and even hostile looking, but with the warm sun pouring down, everything sparkled and just looked cool and inviting. The Queen looked clean and fresh and her smile made her ice-colored eyes look warm.

"Oh, my, " was all Gidley could say.

Casha poked him, in the ribs.

"Come forward, please and state your business with me," Queen Zerena said, and her voice was light and soothing.

They all stepped forward as if in a dream. Well, Gidley and his friends were still awestruck, but Adone and Samal who had been here before, were more poised.

Adone spoke first.

"Your Majesty," he said kneeling, before her. "We have things to discuss with you, concerning our neighbors from Dordom. We have reason to believe that Prince Nekop may be planning an attack and we wondered if you had heard such rumors. I believe you should hear from my friend, Gidley. What *he* tells you may have some bearing on *my* reason for this visit."

Gidley stepped forward and introduced himself and his friends to the Queen. He told her how he and his friends were on a traveling adventure trying to recover a dagger that had been stolen from him. He explained that they believed the dagger was in the possession of Elves from Dordom. He said that they had been told that they might seek food and shelter from her, on their way to Dordom.

Queen Zerena was most interested in what they told her and she called for the captain of her guards.

"Go to Vartu, in secret and find out what you can, about plans that Prince Nekop may be developing for battle. I have not heard such rumors and I must know, as quickly as possible, what he may be up to. Go immediately and take only a few of our guards with you. Nekop must not know of your spying."

"King Handor has heard rumblings, but we don't know anything definite about his plans, either,' Adone told her. Your guards, due to their small size and stealth, may be able to find out that which we were unable to. That is why we came. Also, the dagger may have something to do with all this"

"Now what, about this dagger and what does it possibly have to do with any of Nekops plans?" the Queen asked Gidley.

"I don't know what it has to do with Nekop's plans," Gidley began, "but I know I must get it back. Queen Findra has ordered us to do so."

"Why would Queen Findra be interested, in your stolen dagger?" Queen Zerena asked.

"Well, it's *The Dagger of Bahyel*," Gidley began, "and…"

"What?" screamed Queen Zerena. "If those evil Elves, have taken *that dagger* to Nekop, he must have a plan to do evil with it. We here, and those of you, in Thorpeshire and who knows where else, could be facing a serious battle very soon.

She then told them some things about the dagger that none of them had heard before.

"*The Dagger of Bahyel* was forged, by the ancient wizards, Zowbar and Quindel, in the volcano of Lavors Peak. They put a powerful spell on it and

Nekop would just love to get his hands on it," Queen Zerena said. "With it, he will have the power he never had before and he could do great harm to all our realms. How is it that you come by this dagger?"

Gidley listens to Queen Zerena

"I, I'm a hero. I saved the life of Atilol, and Queen Findra gave it to me," Gidley said, not quite sure why Queen Zerena was looking at him like he was dirt. Suddenly her eyes weren't so warm anymore.

"What I would like to know is, why Queen Findra gave *you* this dagger and didn't explain the great powers and importance that went with it?"

"Well, she said I'd better get it back," Gidley said.

"Get it back?" Queen Zerena laughed. "You are right you had better *get it back!*"

"Yes, ma'am, I'm trying to," Gidley said, shyly. "We have been trailing the thieves, but we keep having problems and it's taking a long time."

"I don't believe this," Queen Zerena said throwing up her hands. "Queen Findra should have sent soldiers to track down these thieves and get the dagger back. Why she would do this, to you, I can't imagine. Maybe she is getting too old and she can't think clearly anymore."

"I'm sure we couldn't say, Casha answered. "About her thinking, I mean. We have been sent and we must find the dagger. It is our quest and it's Gidley's honor we are trying to save."

"My dear girl, if Prince Nekop is doing evil deeds, with your dagger, we are all in trouble. Gidley's honor isn't all you'll have to save."

With that, Queen Zerena called Lea and asked her to show the guests, to a suitable place to make camp for the night and she then turned and went into the palace without another word to them.

Chapter 26

ALL ALONE

Lea showed the travelers where they were to stay and she and several Fairies brought food and vita. The group was also shown where they could bathe, and after they finished eating, they were finally able to make camp and get some much needed sleep.

The following morning, before daybreak, Adone woke Gidley.

"Samal and I feel we need to ride back to Thorpeshire, as quickly as possible, and give the news to King Handor about the power of the dagger, and the probability that Prince Nekop has it in his possession. We may need to start defenses immediately, in order to save Thorpeshire."

"I understand," Gidley told him. "I'm sorry for the problems I have brought on you. I hope you can forgive me."

"We aren't blaming you," Adone told him. "I wish we could stay and help you, but we must get back."

"We will miss you," Gidley said. "Say 'hello' to Dash and tell him I'm sorry. I know you must do your duty and I must do mine. I am well trained and I *will* get that dagger back. It's my fault and I won't let Nekop hurt Thorpeshire or Delightment."

"You may be well trained, but Prince Nekop is treacherous and powerful. He has many soldiers and you shouldn't try to go up against him alone. Wait for Queen Zerena's guards to come back with their report.

She may want to send her soldiers with you, if the news is bad. You'll need help."

"No. I won't endanger anyone else. I'll go alone, today. The others can stay here where it is safe and warm. I'll leave them that way. They have been hurt and put in danger long enough"

"You're a fool, Gidley," Adone told him. "Wait for the Queen's guards. Take them and any other help you need, including your friends, who are also well trained."

"I've made up my mind," said a determined Gidley. "You and Samal better go warn King Handor, just in case I fail or something happens to me. Queen Zerena will know what she has to do by what her guards tell her, and she won't be caught by surprise."

"Why do this alone?" Adone asked, shaking his head and looking at Gidley like he was the world's biggest fool.

"I'm the big hero. I let the dagger get stolen and I want my dagger back!. Please, just go with Samal and let me get out of here without the others knowing. Please, I must spare them," Gidley begged.

"You are too stubborn. I don't know why you insist on going alone," Adone said shaking his head, again.

"I believe Queen Findra sent *me* to recover the dagger, because it's mine and I'm the only one who can recover it," Gidley insisted. "If there is a magic spell cast on it, maybe only the owner can claim it. It doesn't make any sense for Queen Findra to have sent me instead of her army and even Queen Zerena didn't say for me not to go get it. Remember, she said 'you'd better get it back'."

"Then, what use would Prince Nekop have with it?" Adone asked.

"Maybe he knows the way to the power source," Gidley answered.

"Okay, then, you go on, if you feel you must; and it's apparent that you do. Good luck my stubborn, but brave, new friend," Adone said, and gave Gidley a quick hug.

Adone left and Gidley rushed around packing food and his clothes. He took the Special Vita and he took his sword. He worked quickly and quietly, so as not to awaken the others. They would never let him go off by himself.

He started out, while it was still very early in the morning. No one else was up yet. Apparently Adone and Samal had already gone, as Gidley didn't see either of them around.

Gidley made good time alone and had gotten to the town of Sarphe by late afternoon. He took the time to eat and decided he had better try to get closer to Dordom's border before he went to sleep that night.

Gidley made even better time after his stop, and was not far from the border, when night finally fell. As he prepared to settle down for the night, Gidley realized he had forgotten his tent. Luckily for him he was still in Delightment and even though it had gotten colder and he had found the snow again, there was enough magic left in the Fairies' land, to make the night bearable.

He ate and then wrapped himself in his cloak and slept.

The following morning, Gidley awoke and jumped up. A man, fat and jolly, was standing over him saying, "Good-morning, good-morning."

"You scared me half to death!" Gidley said, between gasps of breath.

The fat man stood about three feet tall and was almost as round as he was tall. Gidley knew he was either a Dwarf or a Gnome, because he looked like Mulop and Hebor. Gidley had enough manners to keep that question to himself and he didn't ask, even though he really wanted to know. The fat man didn't have a beard, which Gidley thought was strange, seeing as where all the other Dwarves and Gnomes he knew did have a beard. Of course, he didn't know that many, so maybe this was normal. What he did have was a big round nose and tiny dark eyes and his mouth broke into a big smile when he spoke.

"Oh, so sorry. I came upon you curled, on the ground. Good thing my pony was alert. We would have trampled you," he said. "I thought you might be dead, lying there like that. You're in the road, you know."

"I'm sorry. I didn't know I was in the road. It was dark, when I went to sleep. If you and your pony had stepped on me, I likely would have been hurt," Gidley said, somewhat calmer, now.

"My name is Jessop," the fat man said, extending his hand.

Gidley shook his hand and replied, "I'm Gidley."

"I haven't had breakfast, yet," Jessop told him. "I have provisions. Would you join me?"

"Sure!" Gidley said, glad he had been spared from being trod upon. "Where are you from?"

"I'm from Dawes," Jessop answered, giving Gidley one other answer.

"Oh, I know Mulop, from Lumpor," Gidley told him. "Do you know him?"

"Not personally. I'm from Nebbed, which is west of Lumpor, near the border of Delightment. I certainly have heard of him by reputation. Everyone has heard of him. He is the best archer in Dawes and he makes the bows and arrows for our King Greybar and his army, as well as for the armies of several other realms. You're an Elf aren't you? How do you know Mulop?"

"I was traveling with friends and I met Mulop and he taught us skills, with the bow and arrow," Gidley explained.

"Oh really? Why would someone of Mulop's ability teach *you* archery?" Jessop questioned. "And, where are your friends now?"

"Mulop didn't know me and my friends, at first, but we were introduced through another friend, who helped us," Gidley explained. "And I left my friends back at the palace of Queen Zerena. I'm going to Dordom, to get my dagger back. It was stolen from me, by some evil Elves."

They both sat and began pulling food, from their pouches as they spoke.

"Will you describe this stolen dagger?" Jessop asked Gidley.

"Why?"

"Because, I may have just seen it yesterday," Jessop confessed, as he began to eat. "Please describe it. I may be able to help you."

"Well, it is covered with the rare gem, kimbar, in the shape of a dragon," Gidley began, "and..."

"Stop! Stop! Yes, it is the dagger," Jessop was so excited that he choked on a piece of scone. "You had better explain to me," he said between coughs.

Gidley offered him some vita.

"You have seen my dagger?" Gidley asked, wide-eyed.

"Yes, yes," Jessop said, now that he had stopped coughing. "I was called to Dordom by an Elf, named Zirba. "I was away from my home, when they came to see me. My wife said that five Elves had been there, with a fancy dagger that they wanted me to buy. I deal with daggers, am a historian and an authority, actually. Anyway, she said she saw it and it was beautiful.

Covered with gems, yellow, nice. I say 'I'd better go see this dagger'. She tells me who they were and where they live, so I go there."

"And?" Gidley asked, holding his breath.

Gidley getting the story from Jessop

"And, it is the most beautiful piece I ever lay eyes on. I says, 'this is *The Dagger of Bahyel*. How do you come by this?' cause I know it, I know they can't have gotten it by legitimate means. This guy Bomid, I think. Says 'we won it in a card game'. I think, no, you could not have won this. It is given only to heroes, or the next in line in the family of King Bahyel. It can't be passed any other way. Unless stolen."

"I'm afraid, now, that they may kill me," Jessop continued, "So, I give

143

them a real high price that I would pay them for the dagger, but I tell them I'm not prepared because I didn't bring enough money with me. I never expected, so rare and beautiful a piece. I tell them, 'I'll get more money and I'll meet you back here, in Reld, in one week'. I left as quick as I could. Instead of heading home, by way of the 'Old Sprite Road', I came straight to Delightment, by this road, and made camp when I felt it was safe to do so. I'm on my way to see Queen Zerena, to report the dagger to her. I never felt safe enough to try to make it all the way back to my home. I don't trust those Elves. I feared they might decide that they couldn't trust me not to talk about the dagger, and they might come after me and kill me. Now you tell me your story."

"Oh, well, it's my dagger. *The Dagger of Bahyel* was given to me because I saved the life of Atilol, a hero of Sharrock, where I'm from," Gidley paused for breath. "The night Queen Findra presented it to me was the night of the Winter Ball. Three Elves engaged me in conversation and...," Gidley explained it all to Jessop.

When he reached the part about Dash, Jessop exclaimed, "My, you do travel, in high company. I am humbled, to be having breakfast, with you, Master Gidley."

"Because I know Dash?" Gidley paused and asked. He was confused.

"Dashelle of Thorpeshire. That is who you meant, is it not?"

"Yes," Gidley answered.

" He is great friends with Mulop. Both are master archers. Sorry, go on, please," Jessop pleaded.

Gidley recounted everything else that happened, including the Moards capture of Bellina, the rescue and meeting Adone and Samal and going to see the Queen.

When he finished, Jessop said, "Master Gidley, the dagger you seek has great powers, but the Elves who have it are only interested in the wealth they can get by selling it. They have no idea what it is capable of. Nekop doesn't have it yet, but he will soon hear of it, I fear. Those idiots are telling everyone about it. Nekop has waited a long time to get his hands on that dagger and with it's power he will destroy his sister, Queen Findra, and..."

"What?" Gidley shouted, scaring poor Jessop and his pony. "Queen Findra is the sister of Nekop?"

"Oh, yes. You didn't know? Of course, you didn't or you wouldn't have scared me and the pony, so. Yes, yes, and he knows the power and it's secret. If he gets his hands on it we will all be in peril. He will wage a war to rival all the previous wars. And make no mistake, he will kill Queen Findra."

"I must get it back before Nekop finds out about it. That must be why Queen Findra sent me and my friends to find it. She was afraid the news would spread too fast if soldiers went looking for it. She probably thought, just what happened, some Elves stole it for themselves, not for Nekop. She probably didn't even know they were from Dordom. If I found it and brought it back, no one would know." Gidley finally understood.

"Yes, that must be it," Jessop agreed. "Also, only the rightful heir or hero can get it back. It won't do that group in Reld any good, other than to sell it and get rich. Queen Findra must have thought that."

"What is its history and secret? Do you know?" Gidley asked. "I've gotten bits and pieces from several people, some of whom had never even seen it. Some knew a little history, but no one has told me the whole story."

"Well, okay," Jessop said. "Give me a bit more vita and I'll tell you all that I know. When you get back to Sharrock, you may want to sit with the Queen and get the details that I either don't know or have forgotten. I'm not sure even *I* know the full story."

Chapter 27

THE STORY AT LAST

❦

"Many hundreds of years ago, there were two brothers. Their father, the King, loved the younger one, but despised the older one. The older one was wild and undisciplined and he caused his mother's death. Some say accident, some say murder, because she had punished him for some evil deed. Anyway, the king banished the elder prince to a northern realm, which became Dordom, and set the younger prince up as his sole heir to the throne."

"What were their names? Do you know?" Gidley asked.

"Oh, sure, let me think. The elder prince was Heddon and the youngest was Bahyel. When King Vallard made Bahyel…"

"Sorry to interrupt, but is that where Vallard gets it's name?" Gidley asked.

"Yes, yes and his Queen's name was Sharra, which I believe you'll find is where your homeland gets its name. It was named in her memory. Vallard, Sharrock and what is now Woodglen and part of Kellenshire, was once just Vallard. It got broken up and re-named because of different things, wars, you know. And, of course, Bahyel, you know who that is. Now where was I? Oh, yes. When Vallard made Bahyel his heir, he knew that Heddon would forever cause grief or death for his brother. Because of the disinheritance, you understand."

"Oh," was all Gidley said.

"King Vallard called two masterful wizards, Zowbar and Quindle, and bade them form a dagger that Bahyel could always carry and keep himself safe from his brother. Here is the history, as I know it," explained Jessop.

"The wizards put powerful spells, into the making of that dagger," he continued. "They traveled to Damascus and got the steel and forged the blade in the volcano, at Lavors Peak. They went north, to the Magenta Mountains and mined the gold and the gems for the hilt. They got rubies and emeralds and diamonds for the dagger and the sheath."

"After King Vallard died and Bahyel was crowned king, Bahyel and his brother fought a horrible war. Many Elves were killed; many Fairies were killed. It was the most awful war ever. It is known as the 'Terrible War'." Jessop explained, his hands moving, to convey the drama. "Bahyel was attacked by Heddon, but Bahyel had the dagger and he killed his brother. I hear he almost went mad with grief."

"Go, on," Gidley said, hardly breathing.

"Both brothers had sons. Bahyel's son was Bowdin. Bowdin inherited the land and the dagger. Heddon's son, Mindon, felt his father's hatred for his uncle and cousin, Bowdin. He never forgave his uncle Bahyel for killing his father, or Bowdin, for inheriting everything that he felt should have been his. Do you follow?" Jessop asked Gidley.

"Uh, sure. I think so," Gidley answered.

"Well, Bowdin is Findra's father and Nekop is her brother."

"That would make Bahyel, her Grandfather?" Gidley asked

"Yes, I see you are getting this," Jessop beamed. During the time Bowdin was King, Mindon waged another terrible war and tried to take the land away from Bowdin. Mindon, who had no sons, managed to lure Nekop up to his Realm, Dordom, with the promise of inheriting that land if he fought against his own father. Nekop went. He was mean and greedy."

"Bowdin refused to use the dagger to kill his own son and cousin. Mindon and Nekop tried to kill Bowdin and that's when Atilol, I believe his name is, saved Bowdin. Bowdin rewarded Atilol's bravery with the dagger and bade him always protect his young daughter, Findra."

"Wow," was all Gidley could say.

"The war that you know about, between Findra and Nekop, happened after Bowdin died and is known as 'The Great Elf War'. Nekop tried to take the land that he always believed should have been his at birth, him being younger, you understand, but still being the male child. Atilol fought for Findra, as he was charged by Bowdin, and Atilol's son Andely fought also and would probably have been the next owner of the dagger, but he was killed. There were a good many more Elves and Fairies killed during that war too."

"There's such a mean history between those two lands. It has kept the family divided, for all of their history. And to make matters worse, after the last war, Findra gave land to the Kellenshire Fairies, as a reward for their help, and Nekop has been very angry over that and looking for a reason to wage another war. He has been held back by the power of King Handor, of Thorpeshire and the strong magic, of Queen Zerena, of Delightment. So, now you know the history, as I know it, Master Gidley."

Jessop ended his narrative and took a long drink of vita.

"There is power in that dagger to save who ever owns it?" Gidley asked, not sure he got the story right.

"Oh, yes. Power to save the *owner*, but it must be the rightful owner, presented by heroic deed, or a direct descendant of King Vallard," Jessop explained. "That's why it would be deadly in the hands of Nekop. If he finds some of his own Elves has it, he will kill Findra and take back all the lands that he feels should be his. I don't have to tell you what a bloody war that would bring on," Jessop said, holding his head in his hands.

"I wish Queen Findra had explained more of this to me, instead of giving it to me like she did," Gidley said. "I've been careless, with the one thing that could destroy my home and my Queen and those I love. I'm going now Jessop. Because of your story, you may be the one person responsible for saving us all," Gidley told him.

"It's not me, Master Gidley, it's you who must save us," Jessop said.

"I would appreciate it if, when you get to Fala, you would find my friends and tell them the story you have told me. Explain that I have gone to retrieve the dagger and tell them to go home. I'll meet them there, if I'm successful. They must warn Queen Findra to prepare Sharrock, if I am a failure.

"It's been my pleasure to meet you. You must give yourself more credit, Master Gidley. You wouldn't have the dagger, if you weren't a hero. And Queen Findra must trust you with her life."

"I wish I could believe you," Gidley said. "Take care in your travels and don't fear. I will not let those thieves harm you and your wife. I'll try anyway."

"Goodbye, my new friend," Jessop called to Gidley who grabbed his belongings and walked away, while stuffing things into his pouch.

Gidley turned and waved.

Taking a deep breath, Gidley kept repeating to himself, 'Do not doubt yourself. Be bold'.

Chapter 28

FRIENDS TO THE END

Jessop finished the last of the vita Gidley had left for him and began to pack his own belongings. He soon had his pony loaded and began his trek to Fala, to find Gidley's friends and deliver his message to them.

A short while later, Jessop was surprised to meet up with several young Elves traveling toward Dordom. As he got closer to them, they hailed him.

"Pardon me," said the tall handsome one. "We are on the trail of our friend. We are trying to overtake him. Have you passed him perhaps?"

"What is his name and who are you?" Jessop asked.

"I am Adone. We are seeking a young, blond Elf named Gidley. We were not far behind him, but we were forced to stop for the night near Sarphe, when it became too dark to follow his trail."

"I know your friend," Jessop explained. "I have left him, not an hour ago. He is on his way to Reld, a large town in Dordom. It's not too far, after you leave Delightment. First, I have a story and a message for you, from Gidley."

He jumped off his pony and bade them all sit, while he explained all that he and Gidley had talked about.

The friends listened without interruptions and when Jessop finished his story they all sat looking at each other for a few minutes, while they tried to make sense of all they had been told.

Casha jumped up and spoke first, "We must go to help Gidley. Bellina, how do you feel? Can you finish the trip and fight, if you need too?"

"Yes, the vita and the rest has strengthened me and I've been riding the pony all day. I'll not let Gidley down," Bellina said, also standing.

She knew it was her fault that they had not made better time yesterday. Even riding Adone's pony, she had felt faint and they had to stop often. She did, indeed, feel stronger today.

"I'm well now, too, and I've trained a little with Jinto. I'm pretty good with the bow and arrow," Dira said.

"Gidley will need my sword," Reyal said.

"Me and Miss Bellina, we be a team on them bow and arrows," Jinto added.

"That's right" Bellina said. "We will go protect Gidley."

"Miss, I believe Master Gidley asked you all to go home," Jessop reminded her.

"Oh, no! No! We came with him on this adventure and we stay with him. I'll kill him for sneaking out on us!" Casha said, stamping her foot with each word.

They all could tell she was very angry and knew Gidley was in for a rough time, when she got hold of him.

"Look, it's like this," Adone began, "You all need to go help Gidley. There's a lot more at stake here, than anyone of us first thought. I sent Samal back to Thorpeshire to get Dash. We were to meet them at the end of the mountain pass, between Thorpeshire and Dordom. That's still a good idea, but I feel I should go meet them and everyone else should go find Gidley. We three will be along, as quickly as we can and meet you in Reld. We'll be on ponies so it won't take long. Queen Zerena has already sent soldiers to snoop around Nekop. The less anyone hears or suspects about this, the better. I hope Zerena's Fairies were quick and quiet. As soon as Nekop starts the hunt for the dagger, we are all in great peril. If we get the dagger first, we will end a terrible war before it begins."

"Jessop, ride as fast as you can to Fala, please," Casha begged. "Tell Queen Zerena not to act, unless we are all killed. Gidley must be the one to take control of the dagger. He is the true owner."

Adone said goodbye and left to meet his brothers and direct them to Reld. His pony ran toward the mountain pass.

Everyone else quickly turned toward Dordom and began a fast walk to their friend.

Adone had come to them early yesterday morning, right after he had sent Samal to ride to Thorpeshire, to get Dash. Adone knew he couldn't stop Gidley, and he also sensed that Gidley was right to go after the dagger. Gidley had a need and it was a matter of his pride to get the dagger back. Adone would not interfere with that, but he also knew the others would not want Gidley to go alone; he woke them and offered to go with them to help.

Meanwhile in Reld, Zirba sat in a tavern with Bomid, discussing the wealth they would soon share when the dagger was sold.

Lossard, Drust and Odoman came in soon after, with Lossard's two brothers, Porto and Fromm.

"Somethin' is up with that stupid Elf we swiped the dagger from," Drust began. "We seen that fat Dwarf, who was here to see the dagger, talkin' to him, not an hour ago."

"Did you kill them?" Bomid asked.

"No. Why would we kill them? The fat Dwarf is makin' us rich and the stupid Elf, well, he's just stupid," Lossard told him.

"He's coming this way. We can kill him here, if we want. Besides, I wouldn't dare kill him, in Delightment. Those pesky Fairies know everything," Odoman added.

"Well, boys, drink up!" Zirba told them. "We'll ride out to meet our little friend and kill him. No use anyone else hearing about our dagger, before we get our money."

"What if that fat Dwarf doesn't come back next week with our money?" Drust wanted to know.

"Then we go to Nebbed and kill him, too," Zirba said.

"Then how do we get paid?" asked Losard.

"There are others, who would be interested," Losard was told. "We'll get paid."

"Why not just sell it to Nekop? Why bother with the Dwarf, at all?" Drust asked.

"Because Nekop would involve all of us in a stupid war and we might get hurt or killed. Besides he may believe it belongs to him, anyway, and just take it from us. No. He's the last person I want to see get his hands on *this* dagger. We fell into this quite by accident and we have a chance to become rich, beyond our wildest dreams. Nekop would spoil all that," Zirba explained. "We'll handle this. After all, it's seven to one. We can't lose!"

They all laughed and ordered another round of drinks. This could be fun.

Chapter 29

THE CLASH

As Gidley neared the town of Reld, he found a sheltering tree and ate and rested, for a while. He needed to be fresh in order to fight his best and retrieve the dagger. He had no plan, he just trusted to his luck and skill to be there, when he needed them.

"Do not doubt yourself," he repeated, over and over. "Be bold."

When he had rested, he stowed all of his belongings under the tree and took only his dagger and sword. He was ready.

Gidley entered the town of Reld in mid-afternoon. The town was bigger than Gidley had imagined it would be. There were lots of shops along a wide road that led straight through town.

The main street was muddy, from the previous snow, and well trod by the passing of many Elves and ponies.

"Wow," Gidley said. "This place is not what I expected." After careful consideration he realized he had expected it to be dark and evil. "I'd guess not everyone here is evil, just because the ruler is. They probably don't like him either."

The first Elves that he encountered ignored his question of the whereabouts of Zirba and the other thieves.

'Are they unfriendly or do they just fear Zirba and think I might be one of his friends?' Gidley asked himself. 'Maybe they don't know him or where he and his friends might be. What do I do, if I can't find them here?'

Finally, he asked a young Elf he spotted walking down the street. She pointed to the tavern.

"They always go there," she said.

Standing outside the tavern, Gidley yelled in the door, "Zirba. Come out here and bring my dagger!'

Inside the tavern, Zirba and the others almost fell over laughing.

"Is he really that big of an idiot that he thinks we'll walk out and hand the dagger over?" Bomid asked, laughing.

"I think I'd better do what he says," Zirba told them. Tears ran down his cheeks as he tried to control himself. "He's the big hero. I'm scared." Zirba took a large swig of ale and then spewed it all over Drust, when he couldn't swallow, because he was laughing so hard.

Drust jumped up and would have hit Zirba, but he too was laughing so hard he couldn't even swing his fist.

"Get out here, now, you coward!" Gidley called out.

All chatter and laughter in the tavern stopped and the other customers began to move off to one side of the room. They didn't wish to be involved, with any fight between the stupid Elf outside and the evil group inside. Zirba and his friends would kill you just for what they thought, was a wrong look.

Drust started outside, but Zirba jumped up and pushed him out of the way.

"Coward? I'll kill him with his own dagger!"

Staggering a little from all the ale he had drunk, but still able to walk, Zirba drew the dagger and pushed through the door.

"You're dead Elf," he said.

Gidley stood, with legs slightly apart, his sword held before him with both hands and a look of calm reassurance on his face. 'Do not doubt yourself.'

Zirba wasn't laughing, now.

Bromid, Drust and Lossard appeared at the door behind Zirba.

Gidley didn't flinch, "Give me back the dagger that you stole from me or I'll kill you and *take* it back."

Zirba let out a yell and ran toward Gidley, dagger raised. Behind him, the others pulled their daggers and swords and ran toward Gidley, too.

Gidley stepped back and swung the sword. Zirba jumped away, the heavy blade just missing him by inches.

Lossard raised his sword and ran at Gidley, swinging as he neared him. Gidley jumped back and swung, also. Gidley connected just above the elbow and Lossard dropped his sword and fell down clutching his arm.

Gidley fighting Zirba for the dagger

Zirba came from behind, with the dagger raised, again, but Gidley spun around and hit Zirba on the thigh. Zirba went down and the dagger fell to the ground. It lay there, gleaming in the dirty snow.

Bromid, Drust and Odoman all ran at Gidley at once. Gidley drew back his sword to strike them, but they stopped before they reached him.

Drust fell to the ground screaming. Odoman joined him.

Gidley blinked. There were arrows sticking out of their arms and legs.

Bromid jumped away from a third arrow and found himself, face to face, with a very angry Casha holding her sword before her. As Bomid raised his arms to strike her, Casha let the sword swing. Putting all her power into her arms, she swung from the hips. Her swing connected with the sword Bomid held in his hands, and the impact sent an electric shock all the way to his shoulder. The sword flew out of his hand and flipped over twice in a lazy arc toward earth. It landed point down in the street, and slowly fell over into the mud.

Bomid turned to Casha and she drew back her arm and punched him in the face as hard as she could.

"Good riddance," she said, as he fell face down in the mud next to his sword.

Gidley had run over to help her, but just kissed her on top of the head, when he realized that she didn't need his help. He was about to ask her what everyone was doing here, but Porto and Fromm and several others ran out of the tavern with swords raised.

Reyal fought Porto, but Porto had made a fatal mistake. Reyal was a much better swordsman.

Two more arrows sang out and found their targets.

Gidley picked up the dagger and wiped it off.

The fighting stopped and Gidley spoke, "I see my friends have not let me down."

Holding the dagger aloft he said, "I have my dagger back. A war has been averted. Let's go home."

"Gidley," Adone called, to him. "Come this way. We must hurry to the border of Thorpeshire before Nekop gets here. We have news that he knows of the dagger being here and he comes to get it."

Turning to the crowd milling around, Gidley shouted, "There's garbage, in your streets. Maybe you should clean this place up before Nekop gets here and sees this mess. I doubt if he will be happy."

Gidley grabbed Casha's arm and hurried to where Adone waited for them. Gidley was surprised to see Samal and Dash, bows in hand. They slapped him on the back and tried to hurry him away.

"Come. We have ponies and can get quickly away," Samal said.

"My things are over there, under that tree," Gidley told him. "Let me get them and we can be gone from here."

When he turned, however, Jinto was heading over carrying Gidley's belongings.

Dash reached out his hand to Bellina. "I'm glad you are alright. Samal told me of your ordeal. I'm so glad to see you again."

"Not nearly as glad as I am to see you," Bellina whispered. She felt wonderful, now.

"Okay, love birds, lets go before we have to fight Nekop's army," Adone told them.

"We be doing okay, like, even if we have to fight them," Jinto added.

"Yeah, well, I'm not that good with this bow and arrow yet," Dira, told him. "I'd really rather head to Thorpeshire, if you don't mind."

Dash and two of King Handor's guards had started out from Thorpeshire heading to Delightment to find Samal and Adone, and warn them of the latest news from King Handor's scouts. They had almost gotten to the mountain pass, when they met up with Samal. Dash sent the two guards back to King Handor, with the latest news from Samal. The two guards rode back on one pony and Dash and Samal took the other one with them to carry all the friends, quickly back across the border from Dordom.

They put Casha and Bellina on the pony with Samal. Dash helped Dira up behind him and Gidley rode behind Adone. Jinto and Reyal rode the fourth pony.

Samal led the way as they raced back toward the mountain pass and the safety of Thorpeshire.

Once they had crossed the border into Thorpeshire, they stopped and rested and checked on everyone's state of health after the fight. No one was hurt and they all had a little vita and prepared to go the rest of the way to the town of Durbar, where the three brothers lived. Once there, they would make a report to King Handor.

Dash, Adone and Samal wanted to get a look at the dagger that had caused so much trouble.

They caught their breath when they saw it for the first time. It was exquisite.

"Mulop would certainly love this," Dash said.

"I didn't get the sheath," Gidley said, after a few minutes. "I guess I can use my old one. Just so I have the precious dagger."

"Oh, you mean this old thing?" Reyal laughed, as he tossed the beautiful gem laden sheath to Gidley. "I took it off Zirba. He didn't need it."

They all laughed and a very happy Gidley picked it up tenderly and slid the dagger into it. He fastened it to his belt and beamed with pride.

"I could only hope he'll look at me like that someday," Casha said, sarcastically, and then burst out laughing as Gidley turned bright red.

"Well," Dash said, rising, "We'd better get back to our home. My father will be worried about us and will want to know what happened."

Turning to Bellina, he said, "I hope you'll want to meet him, because I want him to meet you."

Bellina blushed and reached out her hand. "I thought you'd never ask," she said.

"Oh, I have something to ask," Dash said smiling. "Yes, indeed."

A loud chorus of 'aw' greeted this exchange and their friends pelted the pair with little chunks of snow.

"I don't know, but what I won't let Miss Bellina marry you," Jinto said. "She be my bow and arrow partner, like."

"You'll just have to give her away," Dira called out.

"Hey, stop it!" an embarrassed Bellina said. "Dash didn't say anything about marriage."

"Oh, I thought I had," Dash answered.

Bellina stood there speechless.

"Soldiers are coming," Reyal said, pointing.

"Apparently King Handor has sent his soldiers, because he didn't think we could handle this without causing a war," Adone said, laughing.

"Yeah, guess we'd better get to the palace and tell him the story," Samal answered.

Adone and Samal walked out to greet the soldiers and told them what had happened. The captain was glad to hear that the dagger had been recovered and said he and his men would remain behind to guard the border in case Nekop had the intention of following them.

The friends mounted up, as before, and started off toward Durbar and to the palace of King Handor, to report their success.

Chapter 30

REPORT TO THE KING

❦

As the friends rode along, they told each other all the parts of the story that the others had missed.

Dash said he never knew the story of the dagger, other than what he had heard from Mulop and Dorcat that night, in Dawes. When he got back home, he told his father of the meeting with Gidley and his friends and he asked his father about the dagger. His father knew some of the story, but like everyone else with the exception of Jessop, he knew a very little bit and he couldn't be sure of that. *The Dagger of Bahyel* was the best-kept secret anyone had ever heard of.

When his father told Dash that, what he *did know,* was that the dagger in the hands of Nekop would be deadly, Dash decided that he had better go warn his brothers, who had already left their home on a mission for King Handor.

Neither Samal nor Adone knew the story of the dagger before they went to Delightment. Adone heard the story from Jessop, along with the other friends.

Samal still had not heard anything, except what Queen Zerena had told them at the first meeting with Gidley and that wasn't much.

Jinto explained most of what he could remember of Jessop's tale, to Dash and Samal as they rode along, one on each side of him.

At last, they arrived at the palace.

Gidley couldn't help but feel nervous. 'Here we are, at another palace, to tell our story once again,' he thought.

"It's okay Gidley, I'm here and all of us will tell the King the news," Casha said, giving his hand a quick squeeze. "This time, no apologies. This time it's good news. In fact, from now on it's nothing but good news."

'I really have to stop thinking out loud,' Gidley said, to himself. Looking around, he thought, 'Yes, I did it.'

The Friends Meet King Handor

As the group dismounted, several groomsmen appeared and led the ponies away.

King Handor had a beautiful palace made of a light gray stone that appeared to have some sort of sparkly bits embedded in them. The palace was huge, with interesting towers with peaked tops. A red banner with a rearing horse, in gold, crossed with two gold swords waved from the top turret and a coat of arms, with the same image, hung above the door.

Samal, Dash and Adone went to the double doors, intricately carved, and opened them. They bade their friends enter.

A guard was standing just inside the door, but didn't say anything as they all entered. They thought it was strange that they could all just walk in, but then they remembered that the three brothers worked for the King and he was expecting them. They relaxed and followed their friends down a wide hall, hung with gorgeous tapestries. All very intricate and colorful. There were candles everywhere and the cold gray walls bounced the light back, in a warm sort of way.

"There you are, safe and sound. We've been so worried," said a lovely Elf, running to Dash, Samal and Adone. She tried to hug them all at one time.

"Mena," Adone said, "These are our friends." And he introduced them all. "This is Princess Mena, everyone," he explained.

"Come my friends and meet the king. I'm sure he will have many questions. Boid, please, bring food and drink for my friends," Dash called out to a servant who had appeared at that moment.

They all entered the throne room. It was a large room hung, with more beautiful tapestries and, again, that banner with the rearing horse. This time it hung behind the red and gold throne.

King Handor had risen from his throne and was already making his way towards them. He was a handsome Elf, as tall as Dash, with soft, curling, brown hair streaked with gray and a lovely full beard. His eyes were bright and friendly, as was the huge smile on his face.

I'm very thankful that you are all safe," King Handor said, as he took Samal, Adone and Dash, into his arms. "Were you successful in getting back the dagger?"

"Yes, sir," Gidley said.

"Thank you Gidley, for getting back your dagger and saving us from a horrible war," the king added. "I'm assuming you are Gidley. My son gave me a pretty good description of each of you."

Gidley gulped. Casha and Bellina looked at each other. Jinto, Reyal and Dira all realized, at the same time, that their three friends were King Handor's sons!

Boid and several maids arrived, at that moment, and started setting out food and drink for them.

The friends regained their poise just before they made total fools of themselves and relaxing a little, they began to eat.

King Handor had many questions and he gave them all a chance to tell their story. In the end, everyone felt like part of the family and Bellina realized she really might someday, be a part of this family.

'Me, a princess? Me?' she asked herself.

Surprisingly enough, Jinto seemed to get on quite well with Princess Mena and Reyal kept her in stitches, recounting some of their less shining moments.

Casha noticed Dira looking rather sad. She knew that he wasn't jealous of his friends. He was just missing Maye, his girlfriend back in Sharrocktown. She nudged Gidley and whispered that they had better get going first thing in the morning.

"Queen Findra needs to know we are alright and that we have the dagger. We must start for home," Casha warned.

"You're right. I hate to leave our friends, but we do need to get home. I miss Sharrocktown and my little cottage," Gidley said.

Gidley motioned Adone aside and told him they should get some sleep. "We must start for home tomorrow"

Adone offered to show them all to rooms, for what was left of the night. He asked Boid to get food bundles made up for all of his friends by morning.

Dash and Bellina remained behind, talking to the king.

Casha fell asleep that night, planning Bellina's wedding in her head.

Chapter 31

SAYING GOODBYE

The next morning dawned clear and cool. The sun was shining and the snow was almost gone. Gidley woke up feeling better than he had for a month.

He had the precious dagger, his friends were alive and well, and they were starting home today. It was a beautiful morning.

Gidley came down the stairs and a servant pointed him toward the dining hall. Gidley was the first one up and therefore the first to eat.

As you would expect, King Handor's servants had prepared and laid out a wonderful meal. Gidley was amazed at all the different kinds of fruit. And it being winter, he wondered where it all came from.

What he didn't know was that King Handor, like most royals, employed gardeners who worked in a green house all winter in order to supply the royal family with the fruits and vegetables usually found only during summer and fall.

Gidley sat and ate and really enjoyed himself.

Adone came in just as Gidley started on his second helping. Feeling guilty, he started to put the food back.

Adone laughed and told him, "Eat up, my friend. There is plenty."

"Thanks," Gidley said. "I don't usually make such a pig of myself, but today I feel wonderful and everything tastes exceptionally good."

"I imagine it would, after what you've been through," Dash said, as he entered the dining hall.

"Hello. Yes, the weight has been lifted from my shoulders."

"I'll bet it has, my friend. Good news," Dash continued. " Our guards reported that Nekop and his soldiers came down toward Thorpeshire, about a half-hour after we left. They rode down near the mountain pass, but turned west and rode along near the border a short way and then turned and headed back toward Reld."

"Yeah, he obviously saw our soldiers at the border and knew the dagger was gone from him," Adone told him.

"Guess he figured there was no point in a battle, then," Dash laughed.

"Good morning all," Casha called merrily, as she entered the room.

They all rose and welcomed her.

Gidley was glad to see that she was back to her own, cheerful self.

One by one, they all came down, and there was quite a party going on when King Handor and Queen Willa stepped into the hall.

Everyone stopped in mid-sentence.

Queen Willa, introduced by King Handor, told them all to continue their breakfast.

Queen Willa was lovely and they were sure Mena now looked, as her mother had, at that same age. Queen Willa's long blond hair was braided and wrapped around her head, making a rest for the golden crown upon her head. Her deep blue eyes and fair coloring told them where Dash and Mena got their looks. She was dressed simply, in a green gown embroidered with golden flowers.

"I'm sorry I was not here to welcome you after your adventure," the Queen began. "I have been in Sanadula visiting my sister, who had taken ill. She was much better yesterday and I left in the afternoon, for home. Everyone was already asleep, when I arrived."

"It's nice to meet you," They all said.

"I'm very pleased by your efforts, young travelers. You have averted a war," the Queen said.

"Thank you, ma'am, but I'm afraid I had no choice. I started the trouble," Gidley confessed.

"As I understand it, the evil Elves from Dordom started it," the Queen

166

said. "Anyway, it's over now and I suppose everyone will forget the bad and only concentrate on the fact that you are, again, a hero. You all are."

"Eat up," King Handor told them. "When you have finished, we have a special honor for you all before you leave here."

"Oh, no!" Gidley said, looking like someone had just hit him in the stomach. "You aren't giving me another dagger are you?"

They all laughed. Even King Handor, who had a deep, from the belly laugh.

"No. No dagger. You have the only dagger that matters."

"We are proclaiming you all, honorary citizens of Thorpeshire. We have some small gifts, for you to take back home," The Queen said.

"If you all have finished eating I think my son, Samal, would do the honors. Please follow him," King Handor said.

Samal led them to a small room off of the throne room. There, on a table, were beautiful clothes, piled high.

"Try some of these things on. Keep whatever you like. You've been traveling a long time in the few clothes you brought with you. It's time you had a wardrobe that matched your deeds."

"Yes," said Queen Willa. "I wouldn't send you home to be greeted by your Queen and your fellow villagers without having you look your best. They aren't fancy, but they are good quality, befitting young heroes."

"Bellina, in light of my son's obvious love for you and his plan to someday make you his bride, we have a small gift especially for you," Queen Willa said.

Dash held out a gold ring, set with an enormous emerald.

"This ring belonged to my Grandmother," Dash said. "I hope you will wear it and someday be my bride."

Bellina took the ring with shaking hands and she started to cry. "Yes," was all she could say.

"If you're going to cry, you have to give it back," Samal told her and they all laughed.

Bellina surprised him by giving him a big hug.

"You do realize *I'm* the one who wants to marry you, don't you?" Dash asked.

"Yes," was all she could say, again.

"Well, before this gets so mushy that we all lose our breakfast, I believe we have some other things for you," Adone said, happily.

"Oh, yes, come outside," Samal said, as he motioned them to follow him.

Everyone stopped in surprise, as they stepped out the door.

Six groomsmen were standing there with six ponies, laden with bundles.

"One for each of you," Adone said. "You don't have to walk home."

"Oh," said Jinto, running forward. He just realized that the third pony from the left, was *his* pony. The lost pony!

The groomsman led Jinto's pony forward and Jinto threw his arms around him and buried his face in his mane. The pony nuzzled him and snorted. Jinto was happy again.

"I came across him on my way back from Mulop's home," Dash explained. "After crossing the mountains, I cut down through the same field where we first met and I found the pony wandering around. He let me take the reins and I walked him back toward Thorpeshire. I didn't dare ride him, because I knew he was scared and probably very hungry. I gave him my fruit, but I had nothing else to give him until I reached the stable in Vallard. On my way to Mulop's, my pony had started to limp a little and I didn't want to ride him any farther. So, I left him to be cared for by the stablehand there and I decided to walk the rest of the way to Mulop's. That's how I met all of you."

"If I knew he weren't gone, like, I never would a left him alone." Jinto said.

"It's okay, now," Dash said. "We've taken care of him here and I planned to bring him to you in Sharrock. I thought it would be a good way to find out your adventures, see if you had retrieved the dagger and, of course, see Bellina again."

"Yep. No since making the poor pony go through all the traveling we did and them Moards and all. He might a got hurt real bad, like," Jinto added, still hugging the pony.

"Ah, I've never owned a pony," Gidley said.

"I know," Dash said, laughing. "I have to teach you how to ride."

He grabbed Gidley's hand and led him to a fat brown pony.

"Look," Dash said pointing. "This bundle contains a tent. You don't seem to be able to hold on to one for long, according to your fellow travelers."

They all laughed and slapped Gidley on the back.

Soon there after, the six heroes said their good-byes and mounted their new ponies. They turned them southeast, toward Sharrock. They were finally going home.

Chapter 32

THE ROUTE HOME

The friends rode until a little after noontime and were approaching the town of Kudor, when Jinto said, "Don't this be the town them guys, what helped us, live in? You know, when we was under the fir tree."

"It sure is," said Gidley. "We should look them up and return their tinderbox and give them some gifts. They really helped us."

"I'll bet they would love to see the dagger, too," Dira added.

The friends soon came to an inn and everyone went inside to eat and rest. The landlord was a slim Elf, dressed in what the friends now decided, was what all innkeepers wore: shirt, pants and a white apron.

"Just one more thing we learned on this trip," Reyal laughed.

After they had eaten, they asked the Innkeeper if he knew the two men, Elb and Lorge. The innkeeper did know them and directed the travelers to the two houses located just outside of town.

The friends arrived at the first house, but couldn't remember which man lived there.

They all smiled when Lorge opened the door, surprised and happy to see them.

He settled them into his home and offered them food. They explained that they had just eaten, so he got them some vita.

"Let me run down the road and get Elb. He'll kill me, if I tell him I saw you and he didn't. We've discussed our meeting with you and wondered how you made out. Did you find the dagger?" he asked.

"It's right here," Gidley said, patting the sheath.

"Okay, don't show me now. It wouldn't be fair for me to see it without him. We've mentioned it to a few friends and acquaintances and we've gotten differing stories, about it. We sure would like to be able to tell the correct story of how you got it back, when someone asks."

Lorge ran out the door. He returned about ten minutes later, out of breath and practically dragging Elb behind him.

"I couldn't wait to get back here and hear the full story of your adventures and see for myself the wonderful dagger," Lorge explained.

Elb and Lorge sat in rapt attention and never said a word as the friends took turns relating their adventures, since they had last seen the two Elves.

Both Elb and Lorge were amazed by the meeting with Prince Dashell and then the meeting with Princes' Adone and Samal and eventually The King and Queen, themselves.

"As if that's not enough," Lorge said. "We are sitting here, *in my own house*, with the woman who may someday be our Queen!"

The two spellbound Elves said, "Please, let us see the dagger."

Both sucked in their breath, and Bellina feared they might pass out, when the dagger, still in it's gem-laden sheath was laid before them. It sparkled in the sunlight that spilled through the window.

Lorge reached out a tentative hand and looking, at Gidley, asked, "Might I remove it from the sheath?"

"Be my guest," Gidley told them.

"I see why your queen wanted this back," Lorge said.

"Yeah, and I can see why you would do anything to get it back, even staying under that tree like you did, too," Elb replied.

"*That* wasn't our choice," Bellina said evoking laughter from the group.

They all sat around discussing their adventures, until Reyal reminded them that there was a long way still to go, before they reached their home and their own beds.

Reluctantly, the friends prepared to leave. Gidley gave Lorge and Elb some crystals from Mulop's fast becoming empty, bag and returned the firebox that the kind men had given them when they needed it most.

Everyone gave them hugs and thanks and, after they promised to visit each other, all the friends said their final goodbyes and Gidley and his companions headed toward Enod.

It was nightfall when the group reached Enod. The inn they found there was cozy and the landlord fed them well.

The next morning they were off toward Vallard and the Good Elf Village, where they planned to have their lunch and tell Mr. Hymur of their travels and adventures.

The friends rode all morning and a little before noon stopped at the stables in Good Elf to leave the ponies to be rested and fed.

The stableman rushed up to them and started hugging each of them and asking about the dagger and the evil Elves. He said that he was so happy to see them again.

They were a little taken aback by the demonstration of affection and the guys, especially, felt a little awkward.

Gidley, not being one to snub any affection, even if it embarrassed him, threw his arms around the stableman and told him to come to the tavern, as soon as he finished settling the ponies, and hear the full account of their travels.

They left the stableman beaming and promising to hurry along just as soon as he could get there.

"Gidley, you are becoming very tactful and diplomatic," Casha said, teasingly.

"You never know who you might need to help you. I'm trying not to offend anyone until I'm safe at home."

"Oh, so you plan to be mean and spiteful once we get back?" Dira asked.

"No. You know what I meant. Come on, you can smell that soup all the way over here and I'm starving," Gidley said, heading for the tavern.

As soon as Gidley set foot in the door, Mr. Hymur rushed over and gave him a hug, lifting Gidley off his feet.

"Hello, hello! You are safe and return with the dagger. Yes?"

"Yes," said Gidley. Wishing Hymur would put him down before the others got to the door.

Too, late! They all stepped inside, just as Hymur was giving a very embarrassed Gidley, a kiss on the top of his head.

Then it was their turn. Hymur practically carried them to the table.

He drew large tankards of vita and brought fresh warm scones and then returned, with bowls, of fragrant, warm soup.

Eat. Eat, he kept saying and asked several questions and then told them to eat!

They all laughed when Jinto said, "We be tryin' to eat as fast as we can and answering you, like, as soon as we can swallow. Couldn't you be patient one more minute, like?"

"I'm sorry. I just can't wait to hear your story," Mr. Hymur said, as he put more scones on the table.

"Let us eat and we'll tell you the story when the stableman gets here. We saw him first and we promised to wait for him, before we told our tale," Gidley explained. "That way we won't be repeating everything."

"Okay, okay. I'll shut my mouth and … oh, here he is now. Tell your story, Hymur begged. "Good, he has some of the villagers with him. This will be a real party."

And quite a party it was. All the villagers, who had been in the tavern the night the friends first arrived, eventually came in, as the word spread throughout the village that the travelers had returned. Many who weren't there that first night came to hear the story and see the dagger, for they had been told about the quest of the young travelers.

The friends still ended up telling the story several times anyway, and the questions never seemed to stop.

They thought the stableman would cry, when Jinto related how he had lost the pony after the drazil attack.

He looked confused a minute and said, "I could swear that's the same pony in my stable right now."

They explained about Dash bringing the pony to his home and then how they got him back. All clapped their hands at the news. They especially loved the part of the story about the fight in Reld, and cheered when they heard how the friends showed up at the last minute and helped Gidley defeat Zirba and his gang.

"Whyn't you kill 'em? They was bad, for sure," one man asked. "They kilt Henly. You shoulda kilt 'em."

"I'm sorry, but killing them wouldn't have made us any better than they are," Gidley explained.

"Don't worry," Dira laughed. "I'll bet Nekop took care of them for us. You know he wasn't happy with the way things turned out."

"Yeah, I guess you're right," another man said. "No sense you havin' that heavy on your heart. The killin' I mean."

"It was bad enough having to kill those Moards. I really felt *that* was unnecessary," Reyal said.

"I just wish I could have reasoned with them, before the fight started. I was just so scared for Bellina," Casha stated.

Bellina smiled at her friend and said, "Killing isn't right and I'm sorry you have that on your conscience, but they were mean to me and they hurt me. You all did what you felt you had to do to save my life. I'll never forget that and I'll be eternally grateful."

"If I had to, I would have killed those guys in Reld," Gidley said. "It was them or getting the dagger back and preventing a deadly war. I'm glad we didn't have to, but I would have killed them. I was ready to do whatever it took to get the dagger back."

So many people came in, and the friends answered so many questions, and re-told their tale so many times, that it was getting dark outside when Hymur begged them to stay the night.

"We never had much excitement around here," he explained. "Then Henly got murdered, but that was bad. Then you come through, with such a story about the dagger, and we had plenty to talk about. Now you're here, with the very same dagger, the bad Elves will get what is coming to them, and we are all excited and glad to know you are all safe. We may never have this much excitement again. You are heroes."

"Well, if the others want to stay," Gidley said.

"I got a family back home, I'm sure is worried," said Dira. "But one more day or two won't matter at this point, and we shouldn't try to cross that bridge in the dark. It's also snowing a little and I don't want to take another swim."

"I agree," said Casha and turning to the others, asked if they wanted to stay.

They all agreed that they were having a good time and could spend the night.

They had a marvelous evening.

Bellina played the magic flute and Reyal joined in. Some of the villagers played their fiddles and Casha and Jinto sang and then Casha danced with everyone who asked her.

They fell exhausted into the soft, warm beds.

The following morning, Reyal was up before anyone else. He was anxious for them to get on their way.

It was great seeing everyone again and getting to tell of their adventures, but Reyal was getting just a little tired of hearing them all talking and just wanted to go home.

Mrs. Hymur was making breakfast this morning and she brought tea over to Reyal, as soon as he sat down.

"I hear there was quite a welcoming party last night", she said. "Or, rather I should say I *heard* the party last night."

"Sorry if we bothered you. We've been treated well here. We really like Good Elf," Reyal told her. "But I'm impatient to get home."

"I imagine so, dear," She said. "You must miss your family and no matter how good the inn, there's nothing like your own bed."

"Yes. I can't wait."

"I'll get your breakfast," she told him. Hesitating a moment, she turned. "Thank you. You and your friends. It was good what you did."

"You're welcome. I'm glad we were successful."

She smiled and bustled away.

Reyal didn't have long to wait. Just about the time his breakfast arrived, so did all his friends.

"Well, look at this early bird," Bellina said, when she saw Reyal.

"Yeah, we were all being quiet, so as not to wake you," Dira told him.

Mrs. Hymur brought steaming cups of tea. They all sat, with half-opened eyes, trying to find the strength to climb back on those ponies for another five or six hours of riding, before they reached Oakleaf.

They hoped they could make it to Neer by nightfall. Actually, with the threat of lupodes, they hoped to be there long before darkness fell on Galta Forest.

At Reyal's urging, the friends ate rather quickly and soon were upstairs packing their belongings once again.

They soon set their ponies on a course southward, towards Woodglen and the town of Oakleaf.

Reyal was talking about getting back home, but his friends noticed it wasn't Sharrocktown he seemed interested in getting to.

Reyal couldn't wait to get to Neer.

Casha smiled when she remembered the healer, who had tended Reyal's wounds after the lupode attack. 'I'll bet our Reyal was taken with the lovely Miss. Amelli.'

And, of course, Casha was right.

At the palace in Thorpeshire, Reyal had seemed to be interested in Princess Mena. Now, Casha realized that Reyal was charming and handsome and Princess Mena was just another young woman who had noticed that. Reyal wasn't interested in her; she was interested, in him!

Ah, but *he* was smitten by Amelli, and *she* lived in Sharrock!

Reyal had gotten them on the road so early this morning, that it wasn't even noon when they entered Oakleaf.

The landlord remembered Lorge and Elb's tale about finding them under the tree, and all about the unfortunate incident, on the bridge. However, he wanted to hear it again, and this time from the actual participants. He also wanted to know all that happened to them since the last time they were through his town.

The friends related their tale of adventure one more time and when he finally got to see the dagger, the landlord was awed by it.

They told of the ease of crossing the river today: it being daylight, with no storm to hamper their trip.

Their stay for lunch was very quiet. Not many people knew of their quest, when they went through the first time and there weren't many to tell the results of their travels to, coming back this time. All the Elves here were at work in the forest. Everybody needed firewood in the winter, and the Woodglen Elves were busy cutting it for them.

"Can we go now?" an obviously bored Reyal asked.

"Sure," Gidley said, giving his friend a strange look. 'He must really miss his brother,' Gidley thought to himself.

"I think its Amelli he misses, not his brother," Casha answered.

"Oh," Gidley said and smiled. "Oh, now I get it."

They reached Neer just before dusk and were glad no lupodes had been sighted. It was getting cold, and they knew they would have to stay one more night away from home.

"It's just as well," Gidley said. "I'll have to see the Queen as soon as I return and I'm not anxious to do that!"

"Why not?" Casha asked. "You've got the dagger, there is no war. She can only *be* happy. What else do you expect?"

Gidley didn't say anything, he just looked forlorn.

Once the friends reached the 'Silver Bell Inn', Reyal jumped off his pony and ran inside. Very little of the limp that he usually had when he was tired, was evident now.

Murkle welcomed them all inside and when Casha asked after Amelli, he went upstairs to get her. Reyal flashed her a smile of gratitude.

Amelli appeared at the top of the stairs and seeing the group of travelers, broke into a smile of her own.

"Oh, Reyal," she said. "How is your leg?"

"Much better, thanks to you," he told her.

"I'm so glad. I worried about you so. I wish you had stayed here. I mean, or gone home, you know, because of your leg…" she sputtered to a halt and turned red.

Reyal got up and took her hand as she descended the stairs, "Please join us, we have many tales to tell. That's if you care to hear them."

"Yes, yes. I'd love to," she said sitting, somewhat awkwardly, on the very end of the bench next to her father.

The friends told their story one more time.

After a couple of hours, Gidley said that they should be going to bed if they hoped to get home early tomorrow.

"I'm not looking forward to going through Galta Forest," he told Murkle. "Especially after last time!"

Murkle told him that they had only had one lupode sighting since the group had been through last time.

"Either they have all gone back to The Great North Forest or they have all been killed. Two weeks ago, a young traveler from Sanadula, was attacked near the Nork River. He wasn't hurt, him carrying a bow and arrow."

"Well, we have bows and arrows and some fine archers, now. A lupode wouldn't stand a chance against us," Gidley said proudly.

"Yeah and we have swords and swordsmen and a swords-woman," Dira added, laughing.

"And a dagger," they all said.

"You've learned valuable skills and met some wonderful people and learned about some very bad people and strange animals. All-in-all, you have a wonderful tale to tell your children and grandchildren someday," Murkle commented.

"Yeah, we had a pretty amazing time," Gidley said.

"I'm proud to know you all and if I will ever be called on to do anything for any of you, I'll be proud to do it. No questions asked. I'm in your debt forever because of what you did for Atilol and now this adventure." Murkle hugged them all and bade them 'goodnight'.

To Reyal he said, "I'm proud of you and I hope things go well for you and my daughter. She's all I've got and I can see you like her very much. I just want to tell you, I'd be honored if you wanted to court her. You are brave and honest and you have a good trade and will make a good living for her. You put up your life for your friends and I couldn't ask any more character of anyone."

"Thank you, sir. You'll never be sorry."

It had been a quieter night, than last night and Amelli and Murkle were the only people they saw in Neer, both coming and going. It made telling their tale easier. It was nice, because they didn't have to yell, answer a million questions and re-tell each part of the adventure five times.

The group climbed the stairs for the very last night of their travels. They were tired and they had had their fill of foreign places. They were going home.

Chapter 33

HAIL THE HEROES

The next morning Reyal was again up before the others, but this time they noticed he wasn't urging them to get on the road.

This time it was Dira, rushing them about.

"Okay, I've been patient and I've waited around while we basked in the glory from everyone we've met from Thorpeshire to here. I've even waited while Reyal made pretty talk to Amelli. Now *I* want to go home. I miss Maye and I miss my family. Enough already. Let's just go," he begged.

"I guess I'm the only one not wanting to go, now," Reyal said.

"No. I don't want to go either," Gidley confessed.

"Why, for goodness sakes?" Casha demanded. "You were mumbling something about that last night."

"Are you afraid to see the Queen, Gidley?" Bellina whispered to him.

"Yeah, a little, I guess. Me the big hero, scared, again!" he said, embarrassed.

"What are you so scared of? More congratulations? More honors? More praise? You're really something, Gidley," Casha said, shaking her head. "I told you, Queen Findra, will be happy."

"You aren't afraid she'll take back the dagger from you, are you?" Bellina asked.

"Take it away? No. I'm afraid she'll make me keep it," Gidley admitted.

Both of them just stood there and stared at him with their mouths open. For one of those rare moments, neither one had anything to say.

"Come on," Dira shouted.

The Friends return to Sharrock.

"Okay, okay," they all grumbled back to him.

"What am I going to do, when I don't have all of you yelling at me and pushing me around all day?" Gidley asked

No one answered. They all strapped their belongings on the ponies and headed for Sharrocktown.

As the friends got closer to Sharrocktown, Elves along the way started coming out of their homes and waving and shouting to the group.

Questions of 'did you get the dagger?', 'are you home for good?' and 'is everyone okay?', followed them all along the route toward the castle.

The friends stopped frequently, as more and more Elves asked for news.

The ponies were admired, as there were so few of them to go around, and seldom available for the common Elves.

The friends had dressed that morning in the best of the clothes that they had been given by Queen Willa. The friends did not fail to arouse comments of admiration from everyone they passed.

Gidley kept yelling to the villagers, "Come to town tonight. We will relate all our exploits and adventures and we can answer all your questions, then. Now we must get to the palace and see the Queen."

"That's smart, Gidley," Casha told him. "It's better than re-telling our story nine hundred more times."

"I be getting' pretty sick of tellin' how great we done, like," Jinto said.

"Everyone wants to know," Reyal said. "They care about us. We're lucky."

"We're all just tired," Casha said. "I can't wait until I can stay home and sleep as late as I want and eat when I want."

"And bathe," added Bellina.

"I guess Miss. Bellina must be in love," Jinto said. "She never played us home, like, even once. No wonder we be tired."

"I think we're tired, just because we're tired, Jinto," Bellina said. "Besides I played so much that night, in Good Elf, that my lips still hurt."

In a very short time they arrived at the palace and groomsmen came forward and took the tired ponies. A guard opened the palace doors and bade them enter.

"Her Majesty will be very glad you have come home," the guard said.

"Thank you," they all answered.

Queen Findra showed no more reaction, upon seeing them, than if they had just run to Neer for an overnight stay and had now returned.

She looked lovely dressed all in pale green. She even had a veil of pale green covering her hair. It was caught under her crown, and wrapped gently over her shoulders.

"Well, come on in and make your report," Queen Findra said. "I hope you have the dagger."

"Yes, ma'am," Gidley said, kneeling before her and drawing the dagger to show her.

"Arise. I'll need a full report from all of you. We'll go into my private sitting room. I'll have vita brought in."

As she was speaking, several servants entered the room carrying tankards of vita and followed them all into the room.

It was a small room, about ten feet wide by twelve feet long. There were candles in sconces on the walls and the rough stone was covered by lots of tapestries; red tapestries. The candles made them glow like fire and warmed the room.

Everyone relaxed. This was less formal than standing or kneeling in the throne room for what might take hours. And, there was the calming vita.

It crossed Casha's mind that this was the first time that Dira, Jinto and Reyal had been inside the castle and she was reminding herself to congratulate them on their poise and decorum, in the face of the Queen. Then just as suddenly, the thought came that they had been in so many situations lately, nothing should faze them now. After all, they had already met Queen Zerena, traveled and trained with King Handor's sons and had even slept in the castle, at Thorpeshire!

"Are you paying attention?" came Queen Findra's sharp question.

"I'm sorry, your Majesty, I apologize. My mind was wandering. I, we all just want to go home. It's been a long time since we have seen our houses," Casha said, lamely; embarrassed to have been caught daydreaming.

"Okay, let's hear this tale. I haven't got all day."

They told it all, one more time. By this time, they each had a part of the story down so well that they actually paused, when they reached a certain point so the next one could pick up the story from there.

The Queen was very impressed with Bellina's engagement to Prince Dashelle and she even admired the emerald ring Bellina wore. The Queen offered to have the wedding gown made for Bellina, when the time came.

Taking turns, the friends finally got through all their exploits, but the

Queen asked so many questions that they feared they would be here all night.

Finally, it was over and she sent them home; except Gidley. Gidley she asked to stay behind.

Gidley meets with Queen Findra

'Uh, oh,' he thought. 'This is what I've been dreading. I'm in trouble now!'

"What's wrong, Gidley?" she asked him. "You look like you're being sent to the dungeon."

"I don't think I should keep this dagger. I don't want it, Your Majesty. I never should have gotten it. I never really deserved it in the first place and I got it back just by luck. It has a bad…"

"You *must* keep it. It was given to you. You are charged, by me as Queen, to protect me against my enemies," Queen Findra said. "You have no choice."

"But you never told me about the importance of owning it, until it was too late. And even then, as you sent me and my friends off to risk our lives, you still didn't tell me all about it. I, we could have been killed. Begging your pardon, Your Majesty, but why do I still have to protect you? Nekop didn't get the dagger."

"With or without the dagger, Nekop is dangerous and evil. I don't think he's stupid enough to try to get through Thorpeshire or Sanadula to get to me, but I may be wrong. He may be *that* stupid. I just would never underestimate him. Ever!"

Such a look of sadness came over her face that it was heartbreaking to see.

"You miss your brother, don't you?" Gidley asked gently.

"Oh, so you know about that do you? Queen Findra said, as she wiped a tear, from her face.

"I found out a lot of stuff, while I searched for the dagger," he told her.

"No. No, I don't miss him. He never was nice, even as a boy. What I do miss is having a brother who is decent. You know, Gidley, I sense a change in you."

"I think I came back braver, than I was before."

"Braver certainly, and wiser. No, there's another change. I think you grew up since the last time I saw you."

"Is that why you sent me after the dagger? So I would grow up?"

"No. Make no mistake, I sent you because you are the rightful owner of the dagger. Growing up just happened while you searched. You had to get it back. I'm truly sorry, for the troubles you and your friends encountered. I really am. I didn't want you hurt, but you had to face the danger and think about your situation. In order to own the dagger, you must be able to protect it, so it will protect you. I never imagined such a big adventure.

"You should have told me more about it before you gave it to me, just the same."

"Oh, stop whining," Queen Findra snapped, tired of Gidley's foolishness. "Go home, I have no more to discuss with you."

Gidley turned to go.

"And take that dagger, with you!"

Chapter 31

BACK TO NORMAL

A week had gone by, since the friends had returned to Sharrock and Gidley hadn't seen much of Casha and Bellina.

All the female Elves in Sharrock were keeping Casha and Bellina occupied with luncheons, shopping and tea parties. They all wanted to see Bellina's ring and find out about the wedding plans.

All the villagers were buzzing, about Bellina and the Prince of Thorpeshire and there was much giggling about the wedding they knew would soon take place. It seemed everyone wanted to be counted as a friend to the one Elf, who would soon be a real Princess and who might someday be a Queen.

No one could believe the exploits, of these two. Just thinking, about these two tiny creatures fighting with weapons and encountering Moards and drazils and lupodes sent tongues wagging and heads shaking. And if that weren't enough, both Casha and Bellina had ponies; something very few Elves were lucky enough to own and surely not any of the female Elves.

Reyal had gone right to work the very next day, after his return. His brother Levat had several jobs lined up for them to do, as soon as Reyal got back. Levat was tired of carrying the entire work load since Reyal had been gone.

Reyal's parents were glad he was home and were anxious to hear of his adventures and very happy about Amelli. Reyal seemed to think that he and Amelli would marry some day and he wanted his parents, to meet her and her father.

His parents were planning a trip to Neer in the spring season, when the weather was better for traveling.

Dira was happy to get home to his family and his beloved Maye. They had planned to be married in the spring season, after Dira finished his planting. However, these plans were made before he went with Gidley, so Maye told him they could wait until summer, if Dira needed more time. Dira was more than happy to be home and he wanted to marry Maye as they had planned. The sooner, the better, as far as Dira was concerned. He felt he had wasted enough time on his adventuring.

Jinto also went back to work right away. His friend Milo had written down all the requests from the Elves who needed something built or repaired.

He was glad to be home, but he knew he had had a good adventure, overall, and he knew he would feel depressed and bored, if he didn't work.

'I be missin' the travelin',' he thought, to himself.

Gidley was going crazy, just sitting around all day. His only job was to protect Queen Findra and mind the dagger.

He too, missed the travel and the excitement. While it was true that he wasn't happy, *on the trip*, he was even more *unhappy* at home. He couldn't get over a let down feeling.

Gidley hoped that Mulop would come visit him in the spring season. It would be good to see him and show him the dagger and tell him of all their exploits, since the time that they had been a guest in his home. They could shoot arrows. Anything.

'I just have to face it,' he thought. 'Life in Sharrock is boring after all the excitement we had. I thought we had all grown closer, but it seems we've grown apart.'

Gidley felt this way because he hardly ever saw any of his traveling companions.

'They're busy and have no time for me, now. Maybe they resent me for taking them away from their families or for almost getting them killed.'

He also wondered, from time to time, if the others felt the way he did. Maybe they are bored here, too. Maybe they miss the excitement. Or the cold and no food and the danger. No they probably didn't miss any of that.

'Maybe I'll just go off on my own, somewhere. There are lots of *new* friends to visit.'

Gidley spent the whole morning shooting arrows at a board like they did at Mulop's house. He swung his sword and danced around the yard keeping himself limber, as he had learned from Hebor.

'That seems like years ago,' Gidley sighed. 'I think I'll break for lunch. That will give me something to do for a while.'

He looked up just as Reyal came around the corner of his house.

"Oh, good. Someone to talk to," Gidley said, relieved that at least one of his former companions was here and they could talk over their adventure one more time.

He thought it was funny that last week they were all sick of talking about it, now Gidley couldn't wait for someone to ask him about the trip, the dagger, the fights, *any of it.*

"Hey, join me for lunch?" Gidley asked.

"Sure, I need a break," Reyal told him. "I think my brother hates me for leaving him with all the work, and now he's trying to kill me."

"I'm thinking I should learn a trade," Gidley said. "Is it too late for me or can I still get apprenticed, at my age?"

"I imagine you could get someone to take you on," Reyal said. "My brother and I could teach you carpentry. There's plenty of work, if you'd like doing that. Jinto could teach you stonework. He works alone, except for a few jobs that Milo helps him with. He might be glad of a full time helper. You used to help Dira around the farm when you lived with them. Did you like that? They never have enough help, especially in harvest season."

"I wasn't crazy about farm work. The harvest was fun, but the rest of the work was *too much* work," Gidley said laughing. "A lot of it was smelly."

It was the first laughter since he had returned and he was grateful that Reyal had come by.

"Why were you never apprenticed?" Reyal asked him. "You don't have any trade and most young Elves are apprenticed right away, as soon as they are old enough. Why weren't you, do you think?"

"I don't know," Gidley replied. "I guess it's because my parents died. There was no one to show me how to do things. I know I grew up at Dira's house, but they let me help out, rather than teach me a trade. I guess if it hadn't been, for the dagger, I wouldn't have ever done anything."

"Hmmph," was all Reyal said.

While they were eating, both were silent. They both jumped when they heard a knock at the door.

Gidley got up and was surprised to see one of the Queen's guards standing there.

"Master Gidley," he began. "You must come quickly to the palace. Queen Findra needs you immediately."

"Is she alright? She isn't hurt or sick is she? Gidley asked, hurrying out the door.

"She's fine, just come along, quickly"

Gidley was relieved. He hadn't been sure if this protection of the Queen entailed taking care of her during an illness. He wasn't good with sick people.

Reyal joined them.

"Master Gidley," Queen Findra intoned. "I'm very sorry to say that Nekop *is* as stupid, as I feared. I just have received word that his army is trying an attack on Thorpeshire."

Gidley and Reyal nearly fell over.

"No!" was all Gidley said, his eyes wide with fear. "Are they all okay there? How did you find out?"

"I'm the Queen, how do you think I found out? And no, they aren't okay. Nekop is *attacking* them!"

She continued, " I have rounded up my soldiers and some ride to Thorpeshire, even as I speak to you. Gidley, you must fight for *me*, for *Sharrock*. My remaining army will surround Sharrock and try to prevent an invasion if Nekop should get through this far."

"Do I stay here, in Sharrock, or go to Thorpeshire?" Gidley asked.

"Go to Thorpeshire. If there is sufficient aid, Nekop can never reach me. You must kill him. That is an order, by your Queen. You do not have a choice in this matter. We will never be without fear if you do not."

"I thought once I had the dagger safe, again, this would be avoided," Gidley said, sadly.

"Apparently it just made him more determined than ever," the Queen said. "My own brother, and he wants me dead. Stop him, Gidley, please!"

"I'm going also," Reyal said.

The Queen nodded.

Chapter 35

THE RETURN TO THORPESHIRE

Gidley and Reyal raced their ponies back to their homes to get their weapons and supplies.

Gidley had just finished when Casha, Bellina and Jinto appeared at his door. They had ponies, bundles of clothes, food and weapons with them. They were ready to go.

"No!" Gidley said.

"Yes!" the three answered.

Reyal arrived at that moment with his brother Levat, in tow.

Levat was slim, tall and good looking, although not as handsome as Gidley or Reyal. He was about the same height as Reyal, with dark blond hair, which he wore long and pulled to the back in a ponytail. He had bright blue eyes and he was serious and level headed. He had also spent every night since Reyal returned, in the yard at the back of their house, shooting arrows with Jinto or swinging a sword, with Reyal.

"I realize I'm not as good as everyone else, but I need to go with you. It's my duty to my Queen, to protect her and my homeland. Also, I'll not let my brother go have another adventure without me."

"Dira will be along soon. He got the word last and needs to pack," Reyal explained.

Soon, the veteran travelers and one extra brother, were ready to go on another adventure.

This time the friends turned west and headed for the Realm of Kellenshire. They would cross Kellenshire, at the narrowest point, then they would go across Sanadula and into Thorpeshire. This is the route they would have taken on the first trip, if they had known the thieves were from Dordom and had gone back there.

As soon as they reached the border between Kellenshire and Sharrock, approximately one hundred Fairies flew down and buzzed around their heads.

One Fairy hovering, just in front of Gidley's nose, demanded, "Tell your names and state your business. We are at war."

"I'm Gidley and I am Queen Findra's protector. I have *The Dagger of Bahyel*. These are my...."

"Okay, we know about you. You may go."

"Do you need aid?" asked another.

"Nope. We're good. May we stop in Kellenshire to eat, on our way to Sanadula?"

"Yes, you have free passage through Kellenshire. Do you wish to have sentry's accompany you, to stand guard?" the first Fairy asked. "Do you need escort to Thorpeshire?"

"I don't know what I need," Gidley admitted.

"I'll send a couple of Fairies with you on this trip. You may find a need for them during your travels or during battle."

"Thank you," they all said.

Gidley and his friends prepared to ride away, when two Fairies flew over them and hovered there.

"I am Olle and this is my friend Falto. We have been asked to accompany you and give you aid."

The Fairies were only three inches in height, with gossamer wings, which were almost as long as the Fairies were tall. They both had blue eyes and blond, almost white, curly hair and were dressed all in pure white.

"I'm Gidley and these are my friends." Gidley introduced each one to the Fairies.

"We be happy to be havin' you along," Jinto told them.

Jinto was very surprised when the tiny Fairies landed on his pony's head and sat right between his ears. The pony didn't seem to notice them there, so Jinto didn't say anything either. They ended up riding all the way across Sanadula, in the warm comfy mane.

A short while later Gidley asked everyone if they wanted to stop for food. Everyone indicated they were ready for a rest, so they stopped beside the Teld Stream, which they had been following. They had decided they would make better time going that way and then following the Janego River, to where the bridge crossed into Thorpeshire. There they would pick up the road that would take them, into Durbar.

The tiny Fairies joined them for the meal. Both Fairies eating from a small piece of apple that Casha had cut for them.

When everyone had eaten, they mounted up and continued their journey.

They were stopped and challenged by King Sellet's guards and soldiers several times, before they made their way to the bridge. This bridge was identical to the one they had crossed between Woodglen and Vallard. This time there was no problem!

They rode until dark and were just inside Thorpeshire, when Gidley called it a day. He was tired and hungry and couldn't ride another minute.

The scenery in Sanadula had looked just like the scenery, in Sharrock. The land was flat and there were a lot of farms along their route, near the river.

Several farmers had come up to them as they rode by and wished them good luck. A few even offered up sips of cool water, so that they didn't have to stop.

Now in Thorpeshire, the flat land gave way to gentle hills leading to the mountains. What had been a warm, spring like, day was now turning colder, as the sun went down.

Casha and Bellina took the caps off of their flasks and filled them with vita, for the new Fairy companions.

Gidley gave them pieces of scone and Dira broke up pieces of sweet cake for them.

Everyone liked Olle and Falto, but it occurred to Reyal that they were all treating the Fairies like tiny pets.

He whispered to Levat and Dira that they might insult them, fussing over them like that. But the Fairies, having excellent hearing, assured them that they didn't mind in the least being fed by the Elves.

"You look after us, we look after you. You never know when a Fairy may come in handy," Olle told them.

Levat could hardly sleep that night. He was so excited about going on an adventure. All week he had heard Reyal talking about first one, then another new friend or place and Levat had felt so left out. He resolved that if there were ever another trip he would be right there, with his brother. He was scared, but he was determined to have a part to tell in the next story.

The next morning they were all up early and had eaten and packed up the ponies by eight thirty.

Gidley was hurrying, as fast as he could, to aid his friends in Thorpeshire.

Travel that day was easy. The weather was sunny and mild and the road to Durbar was clear and straight. It was probably the most well traveled road they had ever been on. They met Elves every fifteen minutes or so all day.

A few of them asked Gidley and his little army for help, either for food or directions. Most were the elderly and mothers with their children, traveling to a safer haven in Sanadula. They feared the war would spread throughout Thorpeshire, so mothers had taken their children away. Some went to relatives, in Sanadula or Sharrock.

For some of the female Elves, it was the first time they had ever left their homeland. But their husbands were fighting, and the frightened females had no choice except to make the scary journey alone.

The friends were more than happy to offer whatever help they could. They remembered not long ago, traveling strange roads and needing help themselves.

Most of the Elves they encountered found it strange that Casha and Bellina were going, *into* the war zone. And they had weapons!

A few times it was necessary for the Fairies to go with someone, back toward the bridge so they wouldn't get lost or be afraid. The Fairies would then fly back, as quickly as possible, and land on the head of Jinto's pony.

Bellina played the flute as they rode toward Durbar and Dash. She was happy for the first time since they had returned home.

Dira told Gidley, "I never thought I'd ever leave home again once we got back safely, but I've had a restless feeling all week. I knew I had to come with you. I just hope Maye understands."

Thanks, Dira," Gidley said. "I appreciate you being here. You know, I've felt restless all week myself. Yet like you, I couldn't wait, for our first adventure to be over."

"I think it gets in your blood, like," Jinto added.

"Have you felt like we did, too?" Gidley asked.

"I been keepin' myself, as busy as I could," Jinto confessed. "I even be thinkin' I'd go visit Mulop or Hebor or Lorge or somebody. Maybe go see Hymur. That tavern be a fun place."

"Boy, you don't know how good I feel hearing all this," Gidley said smiling. "I've been bored and restless and I thought everyone forgot me and our trip. I guess after all that glory, I couldn't go back to being just plain Gidley, with no fun and adventure. Even the girls weren't around."

"I don't be glad of the war, like," Jinto said. "I just be glad of getting to do something. I don't get much chance to shoot my bow and arrows, while I be buildin' walls."

"How do you think Bellina and I felt? All we were doing was drinking tea and shopping!", Casha exclaimed.

"My brother and I have been working like mad to catch up on all the jobs I was missing, since I left," Reyal said. "You know what? I forgot about the gems we got from Baili Mountain. I'm rich. I don't have to work and neither does Levat."

"Thanks a lot! You never told me you were rich," Levat said, leaning over and giving Reyal a soft punch on the arm. "All I heard about was the sword fighting!"

The friends had indeed forgotten the kimbars. So much had happened since they found their treasure that it had completely slipped their minds.

"I gave mine to my family and some to Maye. In case I didn't come back from the war," Dira said. "I found them when I was packing."

"Well, all mine are still in a small pouch in my room," Reyal said, to Levat. "If something happens to me, make sure you divide them up with mom and dad and Pard.

"What if something happens, to both of us?" Levat asked.

"I guess, whoever makes it back will have to see to it that our families know about the gems," Reyal said.

"We be doin' that if necessary, but you'll both come back. We all be a good fightin' team," Jinto said.

More of this sort of talk took them all the way to Durbar.

Bellina, Casha and Princess Mena console Queen Willa

When they reached the castle of King Handor, they all handed their ponies to the groomsmen and entered the palace.

Levat just stared with a stunned look on his face. Reyal realized that this was his brother's first encounter with royalty and told him, "Stay with me and do what I do."

Levat nodded, grateful that he had someone with him to show him what to do and he didn't have to make a complete fool of himself, alone.

Princess Mena ran down the stairs and welcomed the visitors.

"Oh, I'm so worried," she said crying. "My father and my brothers left yesterday for the mountain pass. That's where the worse fighting is, and my mother and I are waiting for them to return."

I'm sure they'll be fine," Casha told her, putting an arm around her and leading her to a small bench.

"Bellina, I'm sorry," Mena said, when she realized Bellina had a startled look on her face. "I didn't mean to make you upset. I'm sure Dash is fine. They'll be home by nightfall, I'm sure."

"It's okay," Bellina said. "I've got to get used to Dash going off on business for his father. I know he isn't always home. I'll get used to worrying."

"You never get used to worrying, my dear,"

Queen Willa had been told, of the arrival of Gidley and his friends and had come down to greet them. "I normally wouldn't be this upset over their absence, but Handor said they were riding to the Pass to see how things were going and I expected them back last night."

Tears formed in Queen Willa's eyes and Bellina and Mena put their arms around her to comfort her, as she wept for the absent men.

"Huh, humph!" Gidley, loudly cleared his throat and the three women looked over at him. "Ah. Pardon me, but we should go find them. If they are in need of help, we won't do them any good here."

"You're right," Queen Willa said. "It is getting late and you have traveled far. Eat something first and if my husband and sons aren't back by the time you finish, perhaps you should go see if they are all right."

Queen Willa and Princess Mena were introduced to Levat, Olle and Falto and they led them all into the dining room where Boid, the butler, laid out a feast for them.

After they had eaten and rested a bit, Gidley said they should try to get, as far as they could, before nightfall.

"With a hard ride we could make it," Gidley told them. "We need to get going, while it's still light. It's not that far to the border."

Queen Willa didn't think they should go to the battle site. She felt they were too young to get into the war.

Bellina said, "Please, Your Majesty. We should travel closer to where we are needed. It would be nice to stay here safe and warm, but not useful to the war or to your husband and sons. We may even meet them on the way."

"*You* are not going with the rest of the group!" Queen Willa said, shocked that Bellina, a future Princess, would even think of such a thing. "You and Casha will remain here."

"Sorry, Your Majesty," Bellina told her. "I *am* going, with them. They will need my bow and arrows. I'm still a citizen of Sharrock, not Thorpeshire. We were sent by *our* queen, and we came here as a team."

Queen Willa looked as though her lunch was not agreeing with her, but she said nothing as the group left the dining room and headed for the stables. When they had ridden off, toward Dordom, she turned to her daughter and said, "Dash will have his hands full, with *that* little girl. I do wish the future Queen didn't have to be a war hero, too!"

The others in the group, and especially the Fairies, admired Bellina's spunk. She wasn't going to be intimidated by anyone. Not even the Queen of Thorpeshire, who would someday be her mother-in-law!

'Yikes,' thought Gidley. 'If Bellina is becoming *that* aggressive, I'm afraid of what Casha is becoming. She was more aggressive than Bellina, before all this!'

"Just don't cross me and you'll be okay," Casha told a startled Gidley and laughed, when he jumped.

Chapter 36

THE PLAN

Gidley and company had ridden for a few hours, when they spotted riders heading toward them. Gidley pulled his sword from its scabbard and the others, all following his lead, drew their weapons and sat ready.

They were relieved, when they spotted the standard carried by the lead rider. It was the golden horse, on the red background. It was King Handor and his sons.

King Handor and his sons also raised their weapons, as soon as the group came into sight. Who were these people?

Bellina's cry of "Dash!", as she urged her pony forward, let the men know immediately what group approached them.

They broke into smiles and hailed their friends.

The two groups met and all dismounted. There were hugs and back slaps, as they greeted each other.

Levat, Olle and Falto were introduced to King Handor and his sons. Levat was amazed that Reyal knew these Princes' and the King. Not only did he know them, he called them friend and they acknowledged him, as *their* friend.

Jinto built a fire and they all sat down for a talk, about the latest trouble to visit them.

"What has happened?" Gidley asked. "We saw Queen Willa and Princes Mena earlier today and they are very worried about you."

"I know," King Handor said. "We went to oversee the soldiers and give them moral support. They are just barely able to keep the Moards out of Thorpeshire."

"Moards!" Bellina, jumped.

"Yes, Nekop has enlisted the aid of the Moards, from Drog, north of the Magenta Mountains. They number in the thousands and are mean fighters, who will do Nekop's bidding, because he lets them mine the area of the mountains that abuts his Kingdom. In return they give him loyalty in time of war. They help him now," the king explained.

"Nekop won't use his soldiers. Not yet. He keeps his soldiers back from the fighting. He uses the Moards and lets them kill and be killed, until he thinks it's safe for him to use his army. They attack after they have worn down their enemies." Dash added. "Nekop, himself, and his personal guards won't show up until all the fighting is over and then he will ride in, with his standard raised high and complete the take over and get all the glory."

"West of Dordom and bordering Sanadula is a realm known as Hagock. King Zawd rules it. Zawd is friends with Nekop and keeps peace with Dordom by helping him. Apparently he feels it is better to be on Nekop's side, than ours. Zawd too, is using the Moards because there are so many of them and they are expendable. Better the Moards die, than the Elves. The Moards are attacking Thorpeshire and Sanadula, at the same time, trying to draw us out and kill us. Then Nekop and Zawd will have their armies overrun the two Kingdoms and try to take them over. It's only a short way to Sharrock and Queen Findra from here. If they kill her, they take over everything."

"The Moards don't seem to know any better or care, if they die. They just keep coming at us and many of our soldiers are dying," Samal said.

"We got here yesterday and we all had our bows with us. We could stand back, fairly safe from the fighting and shoot arrows, but the more we shot, the more Moards appeared," Dash said. "We didn't do a lot of good, but it let the soldiers know we weren't afraid of getting into the fight. It's important to keep my father safe, however, so we are going back to the castle."

"The soldiers, using swords and battle-axes, are in hand to hand combat. There are many wounded and dead. Every archer we have is busy and I'm afraid we will run low on arrows soon," King Handor said. "We can hold them off somewhat, because the pass is so narrow they can't come through all at once. That is all that saves us. Once they get, into Thorpeshire, they have the advantage of numbers."

"King Sellet is experiencing the same thing in Sanadula. My messengers tell me that King Ryin and King Greybar have sent soldiers down the Old Sprite Road to block any entrance to Delightment. Queen Zerena will use her magic to protect Delightment and probably wouldn't even need help, but it's a show of solidarity of all our nations against Nekop, Zawd and Drog. I'm sure King Ryin has left many Gnomes guarding the pass, into Kimbarton," Handor told them.

"We can only do so much," Samal said.

"Queen Findra has ordered me to kill Nekop," Gidley said. "Is that the answer to this war?"

King Handor said, "All the other kingdoms are peaceful and content with their boundaries. I do not desire more land rule. I hate war, so I would never start one. All the other realms are the same. Only Nekop and his evil followers want war. Nothing is ever enough for them and war is the way to get more. Nekop feels Sharrock should be *his* and he will not stop until it is his."

"What can we do?" Casha asked. "If your soldiers are having a hard time, how can we make a difference?"

"Sir. You didn't answer me. What if I kill Nekop?" Gidley asked again. "Will that stop the war?"

"Yes. I'm sorry, but if Nekop were dead, there would be no use for war. You have *The Dagger of Bahyel. It* always stops the war."

"How will you do it, Gidley?" Dira asked. "You can't break through the Moards. How will you get close enough to Nekop to even use the dagger?"

"He sure isn't going to come here," Adone said. "Not until it's too late."

"Then I'll go *there.* I could go, around Baili Mountain and head up toward Fala. I may be able to get into Dordom there. Then I'd head to Nekop's Palace, in Vartu," Gidley said, pointing out his proposed route on the map. "I'll go through Onom Woods. Nekop isn't trying to get into Delightment, yet. He's got the Moards here and near Sanadula, because he's trying to break through here. It's the quickest way, to Sharrock and Queen Findra. He may think that everyone is so busy defending themselves, they wouldn't try to get to him. Besides, he probably thinks the dagger and I are in Sharrock to defend Queen Findra. I'll bet I can do it!"

"It would take us at least four days, to go all the way around. Why not try going over Baili Mountains?" Dash asked.

"Is there a clear pass I can ride through?" Gidley asked.

"Oh, no. Not over Baili from here," Adone said. "You couldn't take ponies through there."

"If I can't take the pony, I would have to climb up and over on foot. Won't it take just as long that way? Besides, I'd have to walk all the way to Odom Woods and then from there to Vartu," Gidley said.

"Gidley's right," Adone said. "We'll just have to take the four days and hope we get there in time."

"We can ride further than we could walk," Bellina added. "We might be able to eat and ride and save some time."

"I know," Dash said, snapping his fingers. "We will ride as long as we can today, rest ourselves and the ponies tonight, then ride to Lumpor tomorrow. We could get food and more arrows at Mulop's house, then cut down to Nebbed and get on the Old Sprite Road, as Gidley said. But, if we go to Lake Suma we could cut upwards, toward Sarphe, not Fala and go through to Vartu that way. If we really push it, we might make it sooner."

"Yeah, it would cut out a lot of travel through the woods doing that!" Samal added.

"Well, it's Gidley's plan. He has to be the one to decide what we do", Reyal said. What do you think, Gidley?"

"You all keep saying 'we'. Does this mean you are all planning to come with me?" Gidley asked.

"Yes," said everyone, except King Handor.

Gidley threw up his hands in surrender! He knew he couldn't win.

"Do you think it's wise for all of you to go?" the king asked, knowing they all would go, no matter what he thought.

"Please, father," Adone begged. "Give us your blessing. Gidley will need our help." He knew his father could order him and his brothers to stay in Thorpeshire.

"Yes. Yes. Go. Just be careful," Handor said. "Your mother is going to kill me, but, yes, this is important. Go with Gidley."

They all mounted their ponies.

Turning the ponies around, they headed back toward Durbar. A few hours later they again approached the castle of King Handor.

"Goodbye and good luck. We'll hold off the armies here, but hurry. The next few days will be hard for you all, but I'm confident a better group of soldiers can't be found anywhere," Handor told them. "Now get out of here, before your mother finds out what you plan."

Dash grabbed the standard from his father's guard.

"This will give us safe passage", Dash explained. "During war you need to identify yourselves as friendly, right away."

"Goodbye," they all called out as they turned away from the castle and headed east toward Vallard and the pass at Baili Mountain.

Chapter 37

THE REUNION

Gidley and his friends were riding to Kudor where they planned to stop to get food and much need rest.

Gidley felt proud to be leading the little group that would try to accomplish the near impossible. They were trying to stop the war.

The shields of King Handor, in the hands of his sons and the standard raised high, gave them full passage through Thorpeshire.

At Kudor they stopped at the same tavern that they were in last week. Could it only have been one week ago? So much had happened Gidley found it hard to comprehend.

Imagine their surprise when they entered the tavern and heard "Hey!"

Looking over toward the sound, Gidley and the original group broke into smiles. It was Lorge and Elb having their dinner.

They waved Gidley and his friends over and invited them to eat with them.

"What brings you through here?" Elb asked. "I thought you went home?"

"We did, but with the war we had to come back. We're on our way to Dawes," Gidley explained.

"Dawes?" Lorge asked. "Why Dawes? Isn't the fighting here, near the mountain pass and in Sanadula?"

Gidley explained what they had in mind to do. Elb and Lorge were impressed when Gidley introduced them to everyone and they found out they were having dinner, with the three Princes.

"I, I thought it looked like you, but, but, I never thought it would *be* you," Elb stammered.

"Just think of us as Gidley's friends and don't think of us as who we are," Samal laughed. "They don't!"

"Well, it's great we got to see you guys again," Gidley said. "We are pressed for time and really must get out of here. Take care and hopefully we'll see you in a about a week and get to say goodbye, again."

"I'm coming with you," Elb said. "That's if you'll have me, Your Highnesses."

"We Highnesses, have no say in this matter," Dash laughed. "This is Gidley's party. If he doesn't mind, I'm sure I don't."

"In that case I'm coming too," Lorge said. "We can come, can't we Gidley? Me and Elb can't be in the King's regular army. It would be our only chance to help."

"Sure you can come," Gidley told them. "I'm happy to have as many friends with me as I can get."

"Let's go then!"

"Do you think we be makin' it all the way to Vallard, tonight?" Jinto asked.

"I doubt if we'll get to Enod," Dash answered. "I'm exhausted. My brothers and I fought yesterday and today. I'm sure everyone is tired. You guys have had a long ride."

"Why don't you sleep at our houses tonight and we'll all get a fresh start tomorrow," Elb offered.

"We could give the ponies a good rest," Samal told Gidley.

"Yeah, sure. We might as well get a good fresh start tomorrow," Gidley said. "Thanks."

The following morning, true to Samal and Adone's past behavior, everyone was up just about the same time as the sun.

"I can't get used to this," Casha lamented.

"Just hang on to the pony," Samal said, teasing her. "You'll do fine. You can sleep while we ride along."

"I'll be sure to wake you if anything important happens," Adone said, laughing.

"We can follow the road to Enod and eat there, then I know a way to cut up and over Vallard. It will bring us to that field where we first met," Dash said. "It will take almost a day to get through the mountains, because we will have to lead the ponies through some of the rough areas."

"I hope I don't lose my pony again, like," Jinto said, fear in his voice.

"Yeah. What about those drazils?" Bellina asked.

"If there are drazils, I'll shoot them," Dash said. "I'll not let them get you again."

"I be shootin' them, if they try to get my pony," Jinto said firmly.

"That's right, Bellina said. "Jinto and I, will shoot them this time."

"Oh, yeah, *the team!* I forgot," Dash said. "Bellina doesn't need my help anymore."

"Miss Bellina and me do be a team," Jinto said. "That be no lie."

They rode hard and by ten o'clock they were in Enod. The landlord there made a special meal for them, seeing as where the Princes' were with them. He told them that he usually didn't open for food, until at least noon. The group only wanted some scones and fruit and asked the owner to pack some more in bundles to carry with them, as they would not be stopping again, for a while.

There was one other Elf there and he was just having a cup of tea. Gidley thought he looked familiar, but couldn't place him.

Suddenly the Elf jumped up and came over to their table. He was Arry, one of the Elves they had met in Good Elf Village, at the Inn. He had been one of the fiddle players at the party last week. He seemed shy when they had first spoken to him, but found out by the end of the party that he was quite nice and not shy at all. He had dark eyes and shaggy salt and pepper hair that almost covered his ears. His nose was rather sharp and matched his chin.

He was introduced to the group and they told him what they were planning. Well, they didn't exactly tell him the whole plan, but enough to answer his questions and keep him happy.

He said he would tell everyone in Good Elf, that he had seen them and that they would have another party, when they stopped to tell everyone of this tale.

The group was anxious to make the best time possible, so they ate quickly and then mounted up, ready for more grueling hours on the ponies backs.

By five o'clock, they were at the base of Baili Mountain and they stopped long enough to grab a quick bite and feed the ponies. They planned to go, as far as they could, before it got too dark. It was much too dangerous to travel the mountain path at night.

At seven o'clock, tired and literally traveling blind, the group stopped for the night. They all quickly dropped off to sleep. The group was fortunate that the good weather held and it was only mildly cold this night. The two Fairies curled up, in the hood, of Jinto's cloak.

All fourteen of them were up at six o'clock and on the path to Lumpor, after a quick breakfast.

Adone teased them by saying that he and Samal had let them sleep in this morning. Indeed, the sun was up already.

They rode, when they could, and led the ponies when the travel was rough. Still, they were at Mulop's house by nine thirty.

Mulop almost fell over when he opened the door. He grabbed each one in a great exuberant hug and pulled them through the open door. He seemed startled and then laughed, as the fairies flew past him and settled on the arm of a chair.

After they were all settled in front of the fire, and Mulop had pulled all manner of food and drink out for them, he finally sat down.

"Well, do you have it? I'm sure you do," Mulop said.

"Right here," Gidley said, pulling his dagger from its sheath and handing it to Mulop.

"Oh, my, oh my, my, my," Mulop said. "Can I show Dorcat?"

"I'm sorry, but we don't have time this trip, Mulop," Dash told his friend. He then explained their mission and explained why they were there.

Mulop listened to their story and then said, "I'll join you. Do you need arrows? Yes, of course you do. I'll get them. Do you need food? Yes, I'm sure you do. Young ladies, please, pack up whatever food you think we'll need. After I get the arrows, I'll run to Dorcat's home and borrow his pony." We can leave, as soon as I return. Adone, please bank the fire. Dash, grab more bows. We must be well armed."

210

Gidley didn't tell Mulop to stay home. He knew it would break the old Dwarf's heart. Besides, Mulop helped them when they were in need. He taught them all they knew about bows and arrows. Instead he said, "Mulop, I'll ride over with you. I'll show Dorcat the dagger, while we're there. It's the least I can do after his help. We aren't in that big a hurry. Everyone, be ready to ride when we return."

Dash thought how compassionate Gidley was and hoped the duty he had to perform for Queen Findra wouldn't change him. 'He *is* a hero.'

Dorcat was overwhelmed by the dagger and thankful that Gidley had shown it to him. He held it gently in his hands as though he feared it might break.

"I'll borrow my neighbors pony for you, Mulop," Dorcat said, handing the dagger back to Gidley.

"Why? Is something wrong with yours?" Mulop asked.

"No. Oh, no. I'll join you, if you'll have me, Gidley. I can shoot straight and true even though I be old. It's true, huh, Mulop? Mulop taught me many years ago."

"You *want* to come?" Gidley asked.

"Yep. I regretted I let you go alone last time. Isn't that true Mulop?" Dorcat asked. "And if Mulop is going this time, I'm going too. He's my best friend and we sure would love the chance for a good battle. We were told that we were too old to go with the King's army, to Delightment."

"Okay, then," Gidley said, shaking his head. "Get your things packed and get your neighbor's pony and then let's go. Please hurry."

Gidley, Mulop and Dorcat arrived at Mulop's house, just as the other friends were getting on their ponies.

Dash and Samal looked at each other and shook their heads.

"We head for Nebbed," Mulop told them. "That's where we pick up the Old Sprite Road.

A group of four riders were approaching Lumpor, as Gidley and his now large following were leaving Mulop's house. They too were headed for the Old Sprite Road and they tried desperately to catch Gidley and his group.

Chapter 38

THE LIST GROWS

The group pushed the ponies as fast as they would go and arrived in Nebbed around two o'clock.

They stopped only to rest the ponies and Jinto, Samal and Lorge checked each one to make sure they were still in good shape and able to keep up the pace. The ponies were fine and after a quick rest and some water were ready and able to continue.

Gidley was surprised, when he saw Jessop heading toward the stable.

"Jessop, it's me, Gidley," he called.

"Oh, my! Hello," Jessop said. "Did you get the dagger? I wasn't sure what had happened, when I got the news about the war starting."

Yes, we did get it and we went back home. Then Queen Findra found out about the war starting and she said *I* had to stop Nekop. I guess I made him angry, even though he didn't get the dagger. Or I suppose *because* he didn't get the dagger. Anyway, as I said, I have to stop him."

"Stop him? How will you stop him? All the armies, of all the kingdoms, are now fighting him."

"His followers and some of his army are fighting. I doubt if he, personally, is doing anything," Gidley told him.

"You may be right. Yes, that makes sense. Well, I won't hold you. I know you are in a hurry. I'm happy to see you, my friend. Please let me know how you and your friends make out in this war", he said, shaking hands with each of them and wishing them luck. "I wish I could go with you, but I am too fat and getting too old. I do not have the stamina needed for this trip. I would only hold you up. I'm still recuperating from my last trip to Reld. Besides, my wife would kill me if I even mentioned it."

"That's okay," Gidley said laughing. "I'm sure I don't want your wife mad at me! Besides, you helped by giving us the story of the dagger. See you around, my friend."

"Master Gidley, Master Gidley! Wait for us. Please, wait for us!" a voice called.

Turning, Gidley and Dira were the first to realize who the four riders were.

"Hymur?" Gidley asked, incredulously.

"We got word you needed members for your army, to defeat Nekop. We're volunteers," Hymur said proudly.

There was the stableman and Arry, from the tavern in Enod and one other that Gidley remembered from the Good Elf Inn, but had never learned his name.

Adone and Reyal were laughing so hard, they couldn't speak.

"What's wrong with them?" Hymur asked.

"Private joke," Gidley said. "It has nothing to do with you." Shooting them a stern look, he continued, "Okay, everyone. We'll go around and everyone will introduce himself. I can't keep track of everybody, so just introduce yourself and let's go."

They learned that, in addition to Hymur, they would be traveling with Keaty, who was the stableman, Arry, whom they had just seen in Enod, and Wollo. They never did learn, what Arry and Wollo did for a living, but Hymur said they were good with a bow and arrow and knew a little about fighting.

Gidley was afraid he meant bar fighting, but he just smiled and told them to mount up.

Wollo looked younger than the other three and Gidley couldn't remember if he was the one who sang or the one who danced. Maybe he did both. He was tall and slim, with bright green eyes and a crooked grin. He wasn't bad looking, although he looked like he could use a good haircut. Like Arry, his hair was long and bushy. 'Maybe that's the style,' Gidley thought. Gidley was thinking that he hoped the weather held out mild, as none of the four new 'recruits' had on really warm looking clothes. ' I'll have to see if we have extra blankets.'

Hymur apologized, for being the only four available Elves, from Vallard, "But we was the only ones left, with ponies and weapons. Rupert took almost all his soldiers and supplies to Thorpeshire."

Gidley rode up next to Dash, who was leading the way to Old Sprite Road.

"What am I going to do?" Gidley asked. "I hope all these old Elves don't have a heart attack on me. How much help will they be?"

"You know, you're very lucky so many think enough of you to want to follow you into war. They may surprise you. Age and experience comes in handy more times than you may know. Don't count them out."

"I don't mean to sound ungrateful," Gidley said. "I just don't want to be responsible for their deaths."

"They are all looking for one more taste of glory. Maybe when they were younger they went off with some young hero and had an adventure and now they want to relive that time. Maybe they never did anything their whole lives and this is their only chance. Either way, if they die, you can be sure they'll die happy."

"Thanks. I know I can count on you for advice. Okay men. Oh, and Casha and Bellina, let's get to Vartu! We have to stop a war!"

The small army rode until seven o'clock and they all had to stop and get some sleep. It had been a long day. Gidley knew, if he was tired, all the old Elves in his company must be exhausted. He did notice that Dash was probably right about them. They never complained and they all seemed to be so happy. They talked excitedly before they all fell into a deep sleep. Gidley wondered if Mulop and Dorcat had been in the last war?

A shout, from Levat, woke everyone early the next morning.

"There's something standing over there, with a white rag tied to a sword," he said, fear, in his voice.

"Ha," said Bellina. "It's my old pal Lork."

"Oh, yeah, we're on the road right about at where Yanog is located," Gidley said, standing up and walking toward Lork.

"Why do you come back? Do you come back with more men to steal our gems?"

"Don't start that again," Gidley said. "We are going to Vartu to help with the war. Go back up your mountain and leave us alone. We still have the magic flute, and I *will* kill you all this time. I don't have time for your jewel nonsense. Now go away and let us eat. We are in a hurry."

Bellina picked up the flute and put it to her lips.

"Wait!" Lork yelled. "We have seen the soldiers. We believe you."

"Your fellow Moards wage war, for Nekop," Casha called out. "Why shouldn't we kill you now?"

"They are not our fellow Moards," Lork said. "We have left ones like them back in Drog. We have our own colony, now."

"I admire your honor," Grac said, stepping out from behind a rock "You did not lie to us before and you treated us better than we treated your friend. We mean you no harm. Lork, let's go."

Gidley's army was packed and mounted upon their ponies, by seven o'clock.

Samal was grousing, about how late they all slept and how late they were getting started. Dash pointed out to him, quietly, that the older men needed a little more sleep than he did.

"I know, but this is holding us up," he said.

"Let's go," Gidley called out.

They had no plans to stop until they reached Lake Suma.

At one o'clock, they came upon a pony and cart traveling ahead of them, on the road toward Dordom.

As they caught up, the driver turned to see who overtook him. He was so shocked he almost drove his cart, off the road.

"Gidley? Is that really you?"

"Hebor! What are you doing here?" Gidley asked, recognizing the Gnome from Kimbarton.

"I've got a load of swords and daggers, for King Ryin's army. They are at the border of Dordom engaged in a war with Nekop. I take it you didn't get the dagger," Hebor said.

"I *did* get the dagger!" Gidley said, frustrated to learn everyone thought he had failed in his quest. This war was being blamed on him and his friends.

"We go to stop Nekop," Casha said. "Gidley will stop him, with the dagger!"

"May I see it?" Hebor asked, and smiled with pleasure as Gidley laid the beautiful dagger in his hands.

Giving it back to Gidley, Hebor said, "I will come with you, if you will have me. Maybe you need another swordsman? And I have a cart full of weapons."

"What about the army? Won't they need them?" Bellina asked.

"Not if we get to Nekop first!" Hebor told her.

Chapter 39

THE BATTLE

Gidley and his followers had finally reached Onom Woods. They made their final plans for storming the castle and, after a good meal, settled for their last night before the battle.

The following morning they were startled to see Lork, Grac and about thirty other Moards sitting and waiting, for them to wake up.

"We have decided to join you, Gidley. We wish to help punish the ones who have made us leave our old lives and start new ones, in Yanog."

"I thought you had a good life, here, in Baili Mountains," Gidley said.

"We do, but we had to leave our homes and loved ones because of poor leadership. Brec always does what Nekop wants and what Nekop wants is to sacrifice, as many Moards as he can, before he has to endanger any of his own men. He did it before and he does it now. We want him dead," Grac said.

"I understand. We are getting ready to leave. I can't introduce you all now. I don't know, but two of you, and it would take too long. I've got way too many in my army to remember, as it is. We'll discuss the battle plan and introduce you guys, after ward. Okay?"

"We have drazils. Could we give you a ride, to the battle?" Lork asked.

"Ah, no. I think I'll ride my pony," Gidley said. "But you may want to fly above the battlefield. How about bows and arrows? Do you know how to shoot them?"

"No. But how hard can it be? Give us some. We will wage an air war, for you."

And so it began. The war against Nekop. The battle was set.

They all entered Dordom by way of Onom Woods.

Two arrows sang out. The two sentries fell dead. The soldiers guarding the border were vulnerable. They never knew what hit them, as Gidley's army over ran them and headed toward Vartu and the castle.

Gidley's "Army" heading toward Vartu

Nekop, in his castle, was warned of intruders coming toward them, by way of Onom Woods.

He called together his personal guards and rode off to put an end to the breach.

Adone saw a large group of soldiers approaching. The standard, a black dragon on a white field, flying before them, held by the lead rider. They all held shields bearing the same coat of arms.

"Draw bows," Mulop yelled.

Arrows sang out across the field and several soldiers dropped.

Arrows answered and Arry grabbed his arm. He had been wounded.

Casha ran forward and helped the injured man back to safety. She removed the arrow and bound the gash left by the arrow. It had hit high on his arm; his left arm. Arry was right handed and he grabbed a sword.

"I'll not be out of it, on the first shot," he said. "No bow and arrow for me, but I know the sword."

Casha made him stay still long enough to have a drink of vita and then let him go back to the fight.

Reyal was fighting three men. He dodged and swung and dodged and was soon joined by his hero, Hebor.

"Like this!" Hebor yelled, as he swung his sword. Nekop's men fell before his mighty blows.

Reyal joined Hebor and following what his idol did, and what came naturally to him, struck down many enemies.

Bellina, Jinto, Dash and Wollo stood together and showered Nekop's solders with arrows. The arrows flew so fast and true, that the solders didn't have time to draw t*heir* bows to defend themselves.

Grac, Lork and the other Moards in their group, flew high overhead on the backs of the drazils and arrows rained down from above. What Lork said proved to be true; you didn't have to be good with a bow and arrows to do a lot of damage from above. Even if not all the arrows found a target, they kept Nekop's solders on the alert. They didn't know where to turn.

The Moards then flew off toward Reld. They meant to destroy, as many of their former countrymen, as they could.

Hymur drew his sword and rushed to the front line. He was not good enough to make it into Rupert's army, but he would go to his glory, if need be, in Gidley's army.

He swung his sword with glee and moved ahead. He was surprisingly good.

Mulop joined the arrow brigade and with his sure aim, took down many of Nekop's followers.

Casha found herself face to face with a very angry and surprised soldier. She swung, and he died with a look of disbelief on his face.

Hebor, behind her, backed up her every move. Many soldiers in Nekop's army underestimated the power of the tiny female Elf and the old Gnome.

Levat knew he would have a great tale to tell, once he overcame his fear and did what his heart told him was right. Falto landed on his shoulder and let him know whenever anyone approached. They were a good team. Levat wished Falto wouldn't get so excited and beat him on the ear every time he took down an enemy. It was starting to hurt.

Dash, Samal and Adone formed another arrow brigade and tried to protect those who were assaulting the enemy, on foot, with sword and dagger. King Handor would be proud, if he could see how well his sons did in battle.

Keaty, Dira and Lorge fought bravely, their arrows flying straight and true. The many soldiers, who underestimated the surety of their aim, were soon defeated.

Dorcat and Elb worked together and Nekop's men fell before them. Elb was amazed at how well the old Elf was able to move around.

'I'll bet these old guys will be sore tomorrow,' Elb thought.

Gidley swung his sword and worked his way toward where Nekop sat, well away from the action, letting his men die while he watched.

Suddenly Gidley and Nekop met face to face. Gidley was surprised the see that Nekop looked like Queen Findra. He was taller than the Queen, but had the same dark brown hair and he was very good looking. If you didn't know they were brother and sister you might not guess, but knowing, you couldn't miss the resemblance. Gidley had expected to see a dark and menacing figure, like Zirba or Odoman, as though just being mean meant you had to actually *be* dark and menacing.

"You're a coward. You let your solders and the Moards die for you, yet you do nothing to help them win their battle," Gidley said.

"And just who might you be, you little nothing?" Nekop sneered.

"I am the owner of what you wish you had," Gidley proclaimed.

"And just what do you think I want from you," Nekop laughed.

"How about a taste of my sword?" Gidley asked.

"A taste of your sword? I'm not hungry. But maybe you'd like a taste of mine."

Nekop jumped from his pony's back and raised his sword.

"Come on, let me kill you and get this over with. I'm busy with my war," Nekop taunted him.

Gidley swallowed hard and repeated to himself, 'Do not doubt yourself'.

"Okay, we'll fight if you want, but I must warn you, I also have this," Gidley said, pointing to the dagger in it's sheath, tied to his leg. He held the the sword high, as he had been taught my Hebor.

A look of terror crossed Nekop's face when he saw Gidley's dagger, but he recovered quickly and putting as much bravado into his voice as he could, said, "I don't fear *The Dagger of Bahyel*. You, you little fool, will rue the day you challenged me."

With that, Nekop swung his sword with the intention of ending the fight, before it got started.

Gidley was much too quick and agile, however, and Nekop struck at nothing but air. The force of the swing almost took him off his feet.

Gidley didn't wait for Nekop to recover. He swung his sword, large blade humming, and sliced into Nekop's thigh.

Bleeding and very angry, Nekop swung again, this time almost catching his prey.

Gidley again avoided the blade and answered with his own. Nekop was hurt much worse this time. Gidley stepped forward and brought his sword up, hard against Nekop's sword and Nekop's sword broke like a dry twig.

Unarmed except for *his* dagger, Nekop yelled to his solders to help him. Gidley threw down his sword and drew the *Dagger of Bahyel* from it's sheath. "We'll make this even. Don't bother calling for your solders to help you. You know there is a whole history, here, in my hand. You know you can not win."

The Dagger of Bahyel was put, to the test.

The Dagger of Bahyel won.

As soon as Nekop fell, the battle ended.

Nekop's soldiers didn't know what to do next.

Gidley fighting Nekop

Gidley's army, surprisingly, *did* know what to do. They stopped Nekop's solders from any further aggression.

Olle and Falto flew from member to member of Gidley's army delivering messages.

As the fighting ceased, Gidley asked Dash what wounds they had sustained and fearfully, who may have been killed.

Most of the archers were fine, because they were so far back from the fighting. No one could get to them except other archers and no other archers were that good.

Samal had a small cut on his forearm, where he was grazed by an arrow. This happened while he was re-filling his quiver and he was distracted. Adone put some salve and a bandage on it and Samal said he was fine.

Hebor noticed that Casha was bleeding from a small cut on her leg. She looked down in surprise. She never even felt it. Hebor had her sit so he could take a look and was relieved to find that it wasn't deep and required only a bandage.

Levat and Reyal had a few small cuts and abrasions, but they too were fine.

Arry, had not let the wound that he had received way back, at the beginning of the battle, slow him down. He said that he would be proud to tell the tale of how he got *that* scar.

"The others?" Gidley asked, uneasily.

"All okay," Dash said, amazed. "All okay."

They fell to the ground for a rest. Bellina took a swig from her vita pouch and passed it to Mulop. Casha drank and passed hers to Hebor.

"We be the winners, I be thinkin'," Jinto said.

"Yes," said Gidley. "Yes. We be the winners."

"I think we should go to the palace and see if there are others there," Adone said. "What do you think, Gidley?"

"We can't quit, yet," Gidley told him. "Come on everyone. We're going to the palace!"

Chapter 40
THE LAST PIECE OF THE PUZZLE

Gidley and his rag-tag band approached the castle. No soldiers tried to stop them.

Maybe, it was because the air above them was filled with Moards, on the backs of their drazils. Maybe, it was because thousands of Delightment Fairies buzzed their heads. Maybe, it was the line of archers, bows drawn taut and looks of determination on their faces. Or maybe, it was because they knew Gidley had won, with *The Dagger of Bahyel*. No one would stop Gidley.

Gidley pushed open the door of Nekop's palace, and entered.

Reyal, Hebor and Casha were right behind him.

Nekop's servants just stood there with their mouths open.

Gidley was surprised, when a young woman ran to him and fell to her knees. She had long red hair and green eyes. Her skin was a pale white, which seemed to glow in the sunlight streaming through the open door. Gidley wondered where she came from. Not many Elves had her coloring. She was delicate and lovely.

"Please, sir. Help us," she said, sobbing. "We have watched Nekop's defeat from the tower and hope you come to rescue us."

"Who are you?" Gidley asked, taking her hand and helping her rise.

"I am Yanna," she said. "My mistress is Nekop's prisoner. Have you come to free us?"

"Yes," Gidley told her. "Where is your Mistress?"

"She waits upstairs," Yanna told him, pointing toward the stairs.

They mounted the stairs and eventually came to a closed door. Gidley knocked and a voice told him to enter. The woman seated in the room was still beautiful in spite of her gray hair and wrinkles. She wasn't thin and she wasn't fat. Gidley's first thought was that she was comfortable looking, soft and warm and comfortable.

"Ma'am, my name is Gidley. I have defeated Nekop. Your servant tells me that you have been kept prisoner here. Who are you?"

"I am Dorletta, the wife, of King Mindon," the old woman said.

"Oh, Your Majesty, I'm sorry! I didn't know who you were," Gidley said dropping to one knee.

"Arise young man. I am not the queen. No longer. My title was one given through marriage and ended with the death of my husband. Since he gave his realm to Nekop, his nephew, I have been kept a virtual prisoner. Thank you for rescuing me. I saw you in the fight. How were you able to defeat Nekop, so quickly?"

"I have a wonderful army made up of loyal friends, who are great fighters," Gidley said, proudly. "And, *I* have *The Dagger of Bahyel*."

"*The Dagger of Bahyel?*" Dorletta asked, sucking in her breath. "How does one so young come by that?"

Gidley quickly told her a shortened version of the whole story and all that had brought him to this point.

"Your story is fascinating," she told him. "Now what happens?"

"I don't know. Maybe you'll become Queen again."

"No. You don't understand," she told him. "I am no longer Queen. My father wasn't a royal. He was a wealthy merchant and a close friend of King Heddon. They arranged my marriage to King Heddon's son, Mindon," she sighed. "If my daughter were still alive, *she* would be Queen. Alas, she was killed many years ago. I believe by Nekop, but I could never find out for sure."

"Wow! You had a daughter?" Gidley asked. He turned to Reyal and Casha. "Did Jessop mention a daughter? I know he never said anything about Mindon's wife. But then I think the only Queen he mentioned to me was King Vallard's wife, Sharra."

Reyal shrugged his shoulders, "No daughter that I remember, but we heard the story at different times."

"He said, 'no son'," Casha told him. "All he said was 'no son'. I remember that definitely."

"Yeah. That's what he said," Gidley replied. " I took it to mean he had no children. I never thought, of a daughter."

"Yes. That was the problem. Mindon never thought of her either. He wanted a son so badly, that he took Nekop as his heir and disowned his own flesh and blood. Our daughter knew from a young age that her father despised her and when she decided to marry a man her father did not approve of, well, he told her to leave Dordom."

"That must have been very hard on you," Casha said sadly.

"Oh, my dear, it almost killed me. She and her husband sought refuge in Sanadula and when my husband made Nekop his heir, she became fearful and fled to her cousin Findra for protection. When my husband died, she tried to get me out of Dordom. That angered Nekop, and I'm sure that's when Nekop decided to have them killed. The last time I heard from her was when I was taken ill and my servants brought a message from her. My daughter wanted to come get me and bring me back to Sharrock, so that she could tend me."

"I'm so sorry," Gidley said. "My parents were killed in an accident, when I was very young. I know how it feels to lose someone you love."

"Yes, my beautiful daughter should have been Queen, but her father's desire for a son caused her death, as surely as if he plunged the knife into her heart himself. My beautiful Ansella, gone long before her time."

"What a sad story," Gidley exclaimed, tears in his eyes. "I'm sorry for you and Ansella and her husband."

"Gidley! Your mother's name was Ansella, wasn't it? Don't you find that a little weird?" Casha asked.

"I imagine lots of Elf women are named Ansella," he said.

"Not ones, who lived in Sharrock and died at a young age," Casha persisted. "What was Ansella's husband's name?"

"Gidley," Dorletta asked. "Was your father named Havor?"

"Why, yes. How did you guess that?"

"Oh, I just don't believe it!" Casha said, as she slapped herself on the forehead. "Gidley, don't you get it. Ansella, Havor, Sharrock!

229

"How ironic it that?" he asked, shaking his head, then. "Oh! What does that mean? Do you think Nekop killed my parents, too?"

"Could you be my grandson?" Dorletta asked, starting to cry.

"I guess I could, but no. No," Gidley protested, a look of pure bewilderment on his handsome, young face.

"Yes," cried Casha. "It all makes sense now."

Gidley with his Grandmother

"Nothing makes sense, *now,*" Gidley said.

"Of course it does," Casha persisted. "You were never apprenticed out like the other young boys. You did save Atilol, but even you said you couldn't believe that Queen Findra gave *The Dagger of Bahyel* to *you.* We all thought it strange that she made you go get it back from those evil thieves. It was like a test. Once she knew you were brave and had learned fighting skills, she sent you to kill Nekop."

"Maybe she wanted me to find out the truth," Gidley said. "Maybe that's what the quest really was about."

"You must be my grandson," Dorletta said. "I assume Gidley is short, for Gidleron?"

"Yes ma'am."

"Then, yes. Gidleron was King Vallard's father's name. I doubt that anyone would dare name their son after so great a leader, unless he were of royal blood," Dorletta said smiling. She held her arms out and Gidley fell into them, crying.

"Goodness!" Casha said, suddenly realizing what had just been said. "Does that make Gidley the King of Dordom?"

"Yes," Dorletta said. "The true King. Did Findra really never tell you any of this?"

"No, ma'am," Gidley said and he slid all the way down to the floor, his heart trying to escape his chest.

Casha gave him a sip of vita.

"Who raised you? Findra?" Dorletta asked.

"No ma'am. I was raised by my friend Dira's family. His parents were friends of my parents, and when my parents had to go away, they left me there, at Dira's house. We heard there was an accident and that my parents were killed. I just stayed at Dira's house until I was old enough to live on my own."

"Findra never helped you, in any way, as you grew up?" Dorletta asked.

"No ma'am. Not that I know of, anyway. I'd have to ask Dira's parents."

"That's so like her," Dorletta continued. "I suppose I don't blame her, really. The ugliness of this family was here long before Findra or Ansella or even I was born. We had nothing to do with any of it, but it shaped our lives, nonetheless. Yours too as it turns out."

"I don't want to be King," Gidley said. "I don't want to be evil and be expected to kill Queen Findra."

"You don't have any choice, about being King. If you were born a King, then you *are* one. You don't have to continue the bitterness between the families, however. Findra must like and trust you or she never would have given you the dagger. She must have known you wouldn't kill her. Maybe she sensed that you were different, because my daughter was different."

"Yes, but she made me kill Nekop. Now I'm just like everybody else in this family. I have killed my own kin."

"The difference is, you did it because you were ordered to do so, during a war. You killed Nekop to protect Findra, as you had to do, as the owner of the dagger. You didn't kill to gain wealth or lands. You weren't terrorizing your neighbors or waging a war. You didn't do it for your own purpose. You are the first one on this side of the family who didn't. You have broken the curse."

"But I still killed."

"Yes, but you were following orders. War has a different set of rules," Dorletta said kindly. "You must forgive yourself, because you were doing what was right. You must stop this war completely, before many more innocent people are killed."

"Gidley!" Adone called, as he mounted the stairs.

"In here."

"We should go. We need to get to the border of Thorpeshire and drive the Moards and the army from Hagock, away from our friends."

"I must go finish what I started. I'll return and we can see what must be done about what we have learned here today." Gidley kissed the old Elf on her cheek. "We have to get to know each other, Grandmother."

"Grandmother?" Adone asked.

"Tell you later. We have a war to end."

Chapter 41

IN POWER

"Come," Dorletta said. "I will make the announcement to the soldiers. You will need for them to follow you. They weren't able to go against Nekop, but they know who I am and they will believe me when I tell them, who you are."

"Who *are* you?" Adone asked.

Dorletta did indeed make the announcement and everyone who heard was shocked. The soldiers laid down their weapons and knelt, before Gidley. His friends just stood there, in bewildered silence and then all fell to their knees.

"Oh, for goodness sakes!" Gidley said exasperated. "Get up! Everybody, just get up!"

Nekop's captain asked permission to speak to Gidley. He wanted to know what would happen now.

"I, I guess I'm the rightful heir. I am told I am King Mindon's grandson. I guess you work for me now. If any of the solders don't wish to follow me, I suggest you tell them to leave Dordom, right now. Hagock might be more to their liking."

The Captain went back to talk to his troops and several of the guards got on their ponies and rode west, toward Hagock. The Captain, Ponta, came back and said that everyone else would stay with Gidley. He also said that he felt that Gidley should not go into battle. He should stay safe, in Vartu, while they went south to help disperse the evil Moards.

"Nope. I came this far and I mean to end this thing," Gidley told him.

"I have your standard," Captain Ponta said, raising the flag high. Do you wish me to lead us to battle?" He tried to give Gidley the shield bearing the Coat of Arms of Dordom, a background of white with a black dragon on it.

"Are you kidding?" Gidley asked, refusing to take the shield. "If I carry that thing into battle I'll be killed. And put that flag down!"

"Solders," Captain Ponta yelled. "Lay down your shields."

At Gidley's command, his 'army' followed him south, to where the battle still raged. No one there knew of the strange turn of events, in Vartu.

They rode until they reached the area where the armies from Kimbarton and Dawes still held off the Moards, who were trying to get into Delightment.

Mulop and Hebor rode in front, now. They did this so that the soldiers would see them and know that they were not Nekop's solders. Nekop had no Dwarves or Gnomes, in *his* army.

The solders were grateful for the extra help.

Bellina played the magic flute and all the soldiers were steeled for the fight.

They formed up with Gidley's army, in back, and King Ryin and King Greybar's armies, in front. The Moards and the soldiers from Hagock, were soon locked in a losing battle.

They quickly realized they could not win and began to surrender and lay down their arms.

Gidley rode forward, with Hebor and Mulop, and spoke to the captains of the armies, of King Ryin and King Greybar.

They told them of the events that had taken place in Vartu.

Some of the Dwarves and Gnomes were left to stand guard at the border, until all the Moards and the soldiers from Hagock had all left the battlefield and headed toward their home. There would be no prisoners taken.

Some of King Ryin's solders said they would accompany the defeated soldiers and make sure they left the borders of Dordom.

The Delightment Fairies said they would escort the Moards, who wished to remain with Gidley, safely back to Drog. Lork and Grac said they would be happy to help with that.

Raising the Standards

Meanwhile, further south, King Handor's and King Sellet's armies were holding their borders against the onslaught. They were tiring, however, and there were many wounded. Their only hope was Gidley. King Handor doubted that Gidley could do what he promised and he only hoped his sons were not killed in the process.

Gidley and his army and friends got an hour of much needed rest, then he called them all together and told them to eat quickly and mount up. They had to get to Thorpeshire.

Gidley asked the soldiers from Kimbarton and Dawes, who were going with him, to raise their standards and shields high, so the soldiers from Thorpeshire and Sanadula would know they were not the enemy.

Captain Ponta took the Thorpeshire standard from Dash.

They rode south, preceded by the red standard with the golden horse of Thorpeshire, the Grey standard with the white lion, of Kimbarton and the red standard, with boar and crown, of Dawes. Bellina lifted the flute to her lips and played them on toward the battle.

Again, with the soldiers from Thorpeshire and Sanadula pushing the Moards and soldiers from Hagock back into Dordom, and Gidley's army trapping them from behind, it soon became apparent that there would be a full surrender here, also.

In fact, some of Nekop's soldiers were fighting here, and when they realized Nekop's personal guards were fighting against them, they became so confused that they were the ones who surrendered first.

Captain Ponta explained what had happened in Vartu and gave those soldiers, who wanted to leave, the chance to do so. Only a few joined those who were retreating into Hagock.

And so it went, until King Handor and King Sellet's armies were relieved of the battle and the enemies were driven off.

The war was over.

Chapter 42

THE CORONATION

All the friends rushed together and hugged. They were all relieved that the war was over and they had survived.

Gidley and Casha went around to the most severely wounded soldiers and gave them each a small sip, of the 'lifewater', that they had once again brought with them. Thankfully, none of Gidley's group needed any. They headed back through the pass toward Thorpeshire, weary, but happy with the results of their long day.

Samal, Adone and Dash said their farewells and headed back toward Durbar, to give a full report to King Handor. Elb and Lorge said that they would ride with them, as they too, looked forward to getting home.

"You must stop at the castle and meet our parents. You fought bravely and were a factor in the winning of this war," Dash told them. "My father will no doubt wish to give you each a medal for your part, in Nekop's defeat."

"Wow," was all they both said.

Hymur, Arry, Wollo and Keaty said they should get headed back toward home and decided to ride with the men from Thorpeshire, as that way would be the fastest.

"I'd best be gettin' back, before the Missus disowns me," Hymur said. "If she thinks I got killed in the war, she'll sell the Inn and run off with some handsome guy from the village."

Olle and Falto, also, were near home and parted company, with their new friends.

"I can't thank all of you enough," Gidley said. "I couldn't have done any of this without your help. Not just today, but when I met you all for the first time. You each contributed something to my success, both in finding and retrieving the dagger and in this war. I hope once I find out just what this king thing is all about, I can honor you all. I intend to remain friends with you all for life. You can't escape."

They all laughed and said goodbye, with promises to get together soon.

Gidley and the remainder of his group, decided to make camp and rest. They were anxious to get back to their respective homes, but not today. Gidley told Jinto, Bellina, Casha, Reyal, Dira and Levat to go with the others and get back home. Of course, as you can imagine, not one of them did go.

"You'll not be gettin' rid of us so easy, like," Jinto said. "We be findin' out about this king thing, too!"

"Yeah," the rest of his friends said.

When they were near the town of Reld, Mulop, Dorcat and Hebor turned toward the Old Sprite Road and headed home. Mulop invited Hebor to visit him after they had settled down from this trip. Hebor said that he would like that and invited Mulop and Dorcat to Kimbarton, to visit him and his wife.

Gidley was glad that everyone had become friends. 'I'll still need all the help I can get,' he thought.

"Don't worry, Gidley," Casha said. "You will always have me and Bellina."

And so it happened that the original six, along with Levat and Gidley's *real* army, went to Vartu to see Gidley's grandmother and tell her about the outcome of the war.

Several months later:

The servants had been working for weeks to get the palace, in Vartu, ready for all the royals and friends that had been invited to witness Gidley's coronation.

Everything gleamed. Royal bedchambers had been dusted and scrubbed, fruit and berries had started to arrive from royal greenhouses all over the land. Kegs of mead, ale and wine had been gifted to Gidley for his big party.

The Coronation

Many families from Sharrock had begun the journey toward Dordom several days ago and as they arrived they set up tents around the palace and joined the many Elf families from Dordom, who also arrived at the palace gates and set up tents. All were anxious to see the new king begin his reign.

Casha and Bellina had arrived a week ago with Reyal, Levat, Dira and Jinto and all the friends were having the best party ever.

Queen Findra, who was Gidley's cousin and would be the one to actually crown him, had arrived last night with her cousin, Lord Rupert. It was the first time Findra had seen Gidley's grandmother, Dorletta, in many years and they spent long hours talking over the events leading up to this day.

Earlier this morning Mulop, Dorcat, Hebor and his wife, Jessop and his wife, Mrs Baloc, Murkle and his daughter Amelli, Hymur and his wife and several others from Good Elf Village were all welcomed. Elb and Lorge arrived shortly afterward.

All of King Handor's family had arrived at noon, followed by King Ryin and his family and then King Greybar and his family and finally, King Sellet and his family.

Queen Sennabelle and some of her Fairies had gone to Delightment last week, where Queen Zerena was happy to put up her sister and followers for such a happy and momentous event.

At two-o'clock, Captain Ponta and his royal guards escorted Gidley to the palace chapel. Hundreds of candles burned from the sconces all around the room. The strong smell of perfume came from the gift Queen Zerena and her Delightment Fairies had given Gidley; thousands of roses placed in containers around the room and from petals spread all over the chapel floor.

Gidley, resplendent in all black, wearing the royal robe adorned with the black dragon of Dordom, took a deep breath and thought to himself, 'Do not doubt yourself. You can do this' and he walked slowly down the aisle and knelt before Queen Findra.

After several speeches and the reading of royal declarations, the golden crown was placed on Gidley's head and he officially became the King of Dordom.

Queen Findra presented Gidley with the special sword she had commissioned from Hebor, just for the occasion. It wasn't the *Dagger of Bahyel*, but this time it made Gidley really happy to receive something from Queen Findra.

Rising and turning around, Gidley announced, "Let the celebration begin!"

About the Author

First time author, Sandra McPherson, is an award winning pastel artist and photographer. She has been an avid reader all her life and has had a long time dream of one day writing her very own book.

She lives in Taunton, Massachusetts with her husband, Robert "Mac".

19324737R00151

Made in the USA
Middletown, DE
15 April 2015